ONE STEP AWAY FROM

Every man must follow his own destiny...it is all written within us all.

Arturo Mazzeo

Biography

Arturo Mazzeo, class of 1973, is an entrepreneur and writer, he started in the early nineties as a salesman and then opened several companies in Italy and then in London, where he resides today. He has gained experience selling in the internationally, not only in the Italian market but also in the European and American markets, in the fields of services. He has created a series of brands in the pizza, bread, and kitchen sector with which he organizes training courses all over the world, adopting a technique developed by him, leading him to be one of the world leaders in his market, all starting completely from scratch. Today he also deals with the training of sellers in any sector, making use of the techniques acquired in the field from the early 1990s to the constant updates of online marketing, necessary to confront the international market.

Table of Contents

INTRODUCTION

... for those who want more

I started writing this novel between 1996 and 1997, I was about 24 years old, I had been a salesman for almost 4 years and I had recently gone to live in a small studio apartment. I had bought a very small laptop the size of a mini iPad today, I think it was a Toshiba booklet and in that computer I wrote the pages of this book every day. I had already read so many motivational and sales books that had opened my mind and I wanted to write one for myself to begin with, so that I could always remember all those lessons, and then for those who would go on to read it, even if I didn't have many expectations towards those who would eventually buy this book. At first, I didn't have the story or a clear title, I changed it many times before I got the right idea out of nowhere, and slowly writing James's story every day went on and on, as if there was someone inside my head dictating it.

It was 1998 when I finally finished writing it; after which, I sent it to various publishing houses. They all told me that the waiting time for a positive or negative response was about a year. After a year, I received very few responses from publishers and they were all negative…not an encouraging start but, one day a small publisher wrote to me, who I had sent the book to, telling me that he liked it and that he would publish it but at my own expense. It wasn't what I really wanted, but I accepted all the same because he promised me that the novel would be distributed in bookstores by his distributor. I was convinced that if my novel had visibility it could really sell, especially if I could come up with a captivating cover. The cover and title of a book are like the first 5 seconds when you show up for an interview, if you look good you have already done fifty percent of the work and I truly believed that this book could have that. I cared about everything from the choice of the cover photo to the heading, to the blurb written on the back.

The year was 2001, the novel was printed and I had obviously already paid the publishing house, I was looking forward to seeing my novel on the shelf of any bookstore, but the publisher phoned me and told me that his distributor had just called him and told him that he had gone bankrupt and could no longer distribute his books including of course mine. It seemed to me like a scam, of which I could be sure of later by learning about how the publishing industry works. In fact that publisher was just a printer. He had deceived me by making me pay for printing my book, knowing from the beginning that he would never distribute it. All I had to do was drive to his place and get the thousand printed copies and try to propose it myself to some bookstores in my city, something that I never considered.

It was late July and about a week later I would be leaving for my holidays so before I left I put about one two hundred copies in the car and I went around to all the bookstores of my city, to ask if they could take a few copies on consignment and possibly giving me some exposure, in addition I printed a thousand bookmarks with the cover image, the title and a short foreword of the book and gave them to all the libraries who had agreed to take the book. I must say that fortunately they were all available to take it, more or less. Most of the bookstores kept at least one copy displayed in the window. At that time there were no social networking sites, there was only the internet but it didn't have the expansion it has now, and you didn't use Google or another search engine to search for anything.

I returned from vacation in late August and shortly after I went to the various bookstores to see if by any chance I had sold at least one copy of my book. I started with the most important bookstore which was also the largest with whom I had left 50 copies. As soon as I walked in, I went to the place where I knew they were keeping my books on display, it was a pretty visible place where there were also other motivational and sales books, by successful authors, but I couldn't find my books. I immediately thought that they had moved them to a secondary section a few days after I had left them and maybe they had stacked them on some random shelf since I wasn't an important author. I wasn't that disappointed because I didn't think I could sell many copies because no one knew me, so I thought to myself: "why would someone spend 15 euros on my book when they could buy a book by a famous author at the same price? It's normal that I didn't sell anything." I called the store manager and asked her where they had moved my books to and she said "we didn't move them all!" I was in disbelief and looking at her, even she was astonished by this respone. She paid me for the copies she sold and asked me to bring her another fifty. I couldn't believe it; I had sold fifty books in twenty days and they had asked for another fifty. I continued the tour of the other bookstores and also in the others I had sold all the copies I had left ,or there were very few left,and all libraries asked me to bring back more copies. I would restock all the bookstores and about once a month or so I would go to resupply them or sometimes they would call me to ask me to bring back more copies because they were all out.

After a few months the copies I had printed were sold out and I sent the book to another publishing house to print the second edition, but only to have a brand of a publisher on the cover, to give it a more professional look, because I was aware that I would need to take care of the distribution and promotion myself. The first years during the Christmas period I had to go to the bookstores to stock the book 3 or 4 times, they told me that there were people who bought more copies to give away and I thought "I cannot believe that someone is going to receive my book as Christmas present." There have been many anecdotes that have struck me that still today I can't explain. I wrote this book for myself, to help me in times of difficulty, and I believed that I had written a book that could only interest those who are self employed, those who are salesman or those who want to do something enterprising in their lives.

Instead, they began emailing me, a series of people who had nothing to do with my world, people of all ages, from the most diverse jobs, from a bank clerk, to the supermarket cashier, to a social worker, to thank me for writing this book and to tell me above all that this book had helped them overcome a difficult time. One time a lady told me that after reading this book, she stopped mourning for her father's death, and that this book gave her the strength to overcome this loss. People who told me that they had read the book more than ten times, people who told me that they always keep it in their bedside table, people who told me that they always keep it in their bag, who told me thatthey have highlighted many parts and that every so often they read it again. There were those who wanted to meet me, to talk to me, to ask me for advice.

Actually I didn't feel like I measured up to take on the responsibilities they attributed to me. Even today I don't feel like a guru or an old sage. I didn't feel like I wrote things that could reach people of various kinds so deeply, and I honestly didn't know what to say to all those people, I even felt uncomfortable. Once while resupplying one of the bookstores, the manager told me that a person had recently purchased twenty copies of my book to give away during a motivational sales course. I didn't know who that person was, but a year later he contacted me to invite me to one of his seminars, and when I showed up, he was amazed to see how young I was back then, perhaps he expected that for the kind of novel I had written I had to be at least middle aged.

I also proposed the book to a chain of supermarket bookstores, Coop Central Italy, and they said "let's give a try, since you are a local author, give us ten copies. If they sell, we will take more", then I replied that there were no problems but as long as they did not put them among the local authors because I do not write folk or dialect tales otherwise they would not sell. If they had given me the right placement, I would have sold them, as it happened and it was going on with the other bookstores. They then gave me free rein and said "position them yourself with the department manager, put them wherever you want". I put it next to books by famous, successful motivational authors and my book began to be sold at Coop.

One day a friend of mine who still didn't believe much in what was happening told me that he changed is mind when one day he was standing in line at the checkout of a bookstore in another city and in front of him a guy asked the cashier if they had the book "A Step from the Cloud" by Arturo Mazzeo. The cashier, who didn't know me checked the computer and said "sorry no" and that maybe she could order it. At that moment my friend really realized what was happening.

The bookstores of my city knew me by then and told me that it had never happened in all its many years to see a book by a local author, self-produced that for years sold almost like books by famous authors from important publishing houses and could not explain why.

After "A step from the clouds" I also published 4 more books and after five years I slowly began taking on other projects and work commitments that took me abroad, I began to reduce my presence in bookstores; until a day after bringing copies to the larger bookstore for the umpteenth time, where it can be said that it all started, I decided to take a break.

The satisfaction I took, considering how this adventure in the bookstore had begun, without distributor with a thousand copies to sell on my own. I was convinced, however, that as I had been successful in my small local town, whether I had the chance to propose myself to the national or international sphere maybe I could sell my books there too, but at that time I did not know how to do it and the means that we have today didn't exist. It's been more than twenty years since I wrote "A Step from the Clouds" in that small studio apartment and since that time I've done a myriad of things, that I could have never imagined. Today I have become a sort of "James Jaspersen", in another field; you will find out who James Jaspersen is by reading this book. This book is the result of who I was and what I was thinking at twenty-four years old, obviously if I had written this book today it would be different because it would be the result of other life experiences and knowledge. However, I wanted to present the book again, almost the same way it was when it was first published, just correcting some stylistic and orthographic errors and added some small thoughts in order to enrich it, but remaining faithful to the story that had been appreciated by all those who had purchased it at its release. Now I will leave you James Jaspersen's tale, who's waiting for you. Enjoy your reading.

PREMISE

Dreams are nothing more than cues
that our mind gives us to make us
turn them into reality.

(Arturo Mazzeo)

It was wonderful to watch the few lights still lit in the skyscrapers that lit up like stars on a Manhattan night.

Who knows how many times James had stopped to contemplate them, but that night, for a strange reason he was reliving the same emotion as when he first arrived in New York many years before.

This unexpected feeling made him melancholic and he was reminded of his entire past, retracing like a flash back the road that had brought him there and this moved him.

A good book in my opinion, should be read as you smoke a good cigar enjoying the intense aroma that sticks in your mouth, before blowing out the smoke.

This book is about a journey, a long journey, the longest a man can make... the one within himself.

It is the only trip that knows no boundaries, the only one that does not need a boarding pass, the only one able to make us go back in time, to meet lost people again, desired faces and faces that we would rather forget.

A journey in which you go in the spasmodic search of yourself, searching for something that will never turn into certainty.

"How are we really made?"

"Why are we here?"

"Why do certain circumstances happen?"

To these questions James drew his personal conclusion: that we are part of someone's project, because by analyzing the processes of their lives, everyone can understand, even if not immediately, that everything eventually happens for a precise purpose.

In life you have to do things before to understand others later, and if you didn't do the previous ones that seemed wrong you wouldn't be able to understand what you understood afterwards. Everything is a cycle that ends until you get to the final conclusion, until you understand why you came into the world, until you reach your true goal. Each of us has a very specific purpose here, each one of us is like a piece of a puzzle, we are all intersected with each other, we are all interconnected, I am useful to you, you are useful to me, even if we do not know how or why.

Every encounter we make in life is not random, each of us serves a purpose, through our actions we trigger positive or negative emotions that change lives, we unintentionally make other people understand things and vice versa, others have the same effect on us.

We often ask ourselves "if I hadn't done this or that," but you did, and all of this has caused small or big changes to you and to the people you've involved in your actions.

The consequences of every action we make, make those who we involve in our course of action understand things, giving them a higher degree of awareness in life.

In every phase of our life, we act in a different way, facing the same situation, because of our never ending interior evolution. Everything we do after changing ourselves, we do it differently than before so as a result what we do from then on, will have different consequences from the actions we would have committed if we hadn't changed because of what we had done before.

This is the cycle of our whole lives; it is full of continuous changes, internal change due to the actions provoked by us and others that are interconnected with us. As a result we act differently, when facing the same situation, because of what happened to us in the past. We are always conditioned by what happened in the past. The fears we have today are caused by past traumas, otherwise we would not have many of the fears we have now. A child is fearless, because he doesn't have past experience to rely on.

Based on the same event, each draws different conclusions, that will condition their future.

Every time you receive some new information in your life, it causes you to change and every time you change, you're not the same person as before. That's why when facing the same situation another time, you'll behave differently than you have done before.

Only by overcoming critical moments can one discover the dark aspects of one's character and have the opportunity to improve oneself.

Once learnt this philosophy, James as a masochisit began to voluntarily get into trouble whenever he was thirsty for new teachings of life. Whenever he wanted to understand the extent to which he was strong or when he felt the need to change direction in his life. There are those who constantly flee from trouble by protecting themselves in their comfort zone tending to always stay in their own environment and with the same people, because this makes them feel protected and those who instead tend to get out of their comfort zone to explore the world and challenge themselves with different realities that can enrich themselves by inevitably triggering internal changes.

If you want to get to know yourself well and you want to understand who you really are and how far you can get, you need to leave your comfort zone. The more you are willing to leave your comfort zone the more you change and each change will make you behave differently, and each action will result in consequences that will lead you to explore new paths that will lead you to a goal that you did not initially consider.

If for example a set of twin brothers grow up together and then one of them decides to leave their shared comfort zone then after years. If one of them continues to stay out of it with the consequences of being irretrievably changed many times and no longer being the same person as they were before, when he sees his twin brother again and what he once was, but he will no longer recognize himself in that person and the comfortable environment he had left behind and will feel alien.

You're about to read what James Jaspersen wrote that night, the night he paused to look at the few lights left still on, in Manhattan's skyscrapers, looking at that scenery sitting in his aged brown leather armchair in front of his desk he realized more and more how anything is really possible in life if you get out of your comfort zone.

It is the diary of his life written freehand in a moment, like a long and deep report, surrounded by reflections and opinions on more disparate topics, until we arrive at a surprise double finale.

This book encompasses a point of view that is not necessarily expected to be shared, because it expresses a point of view on life and it must be judged as such.

I would like to call it a motivational book because by identifying with the protagonist, taking inspiration from his ideas and how he has solved certain situations, it could be a form of encouragement for someone who is in a similar situation.

If even for a moment reading this book you will be able to feel "a step away from the clouds", at that moment we will be together and my purpose will be achieved.

CHAPTER ONE

*Your current living conditions
do not indicate what you will be in the future.
Don't let your current
living conditions affect you*

(Arturo Mazzeo)

It would have been easy to enter that silent office where only the hum of a lit printer and the rustle of a computer processing data, could disturb the afternoon silence; look him in the eye and say, in a discounted tone of voice, "I've decided to stay!"

It would have been easy to enter that office, personalized with small frames hanging on the white walls, where under glass were enclosed phrases such as: "there is only one way to live happily: to live as you want"; look at him with an obvious grimace, symbolizing: "You were right", and say to him: "I have decided to stay!".

It would have been difficult to deceive myself if I hadn't found the courage to say "I can't stay!" in front of his enchanting magical eyes.

I knew that the fundamental reason for all those people who have reached the decline that are reaching it is to have rested on their laurels. The most critical moment of a man's path to improvement occurs when things are going well, because blinded by the past achievements, they no longer seek new ways of improving themselves and stubbornly carry on those models of success that in the long run will show their second face: failure.

Life is all about cycles. You always have to monitor.

I mean you have to follow the changes of society if you want to be one of the protagonists and not just a spectator.

If one thing is right today, who's to say that it will be right tomorrow.

It is instinctual of man not to give up the winning formula that has proved him successful in the past; but to find new horizons, it is essential to know how to question the formula of one's own success.

The seeds of failure are varied, but all linked to the natural tendency to continue to do what is well done without confronting those who are building new roads.

For this reason, success is sometimes an obstacle to change, a change understood as improvement.

Generally, you tend to change when the phase of decline comes, but unfortunately at that point it is already too late.

But it's hard to tell when the exact time to change is... Something that I have always whispered to myself, and often the people who knew me thought I was just insane and often said"James but what you do is going all right! Why do you want to change?"It's like when a boxer gets older and understands it's time to retire if he doesn't want the last fight to be the one that takes his life. But believe me, when you're successful in doing something and it also earns you money even if you sense that in that industry there's a decline, as long as you're gaining it's hard to think that sooner or later the revenue will end and you think maybe it's going to happen to others and not to you because you're better. But then one day when you start to see that suddenly there is a turnaround and your revenue starts to no longer be the same, it's starting to be too late to save you if you had not already activated a plan B. You always have to have a plan B and also a plan C but not in your head, they must already be perfectly planned and feasible right away. Theoretical B plans are of no use, they are only dreams. You have to have a plan B already tested and implemented by yourself and not by others.

When I left my post at Golden Shoes, I did it after a time when the mirror reflected an image I no longer valued. I kept visiting the usual customers so I didn't have any interest anymore, I was just tired of having to do the same things all the time.

I have heard that the easiest way to deal with problems is not to deal with them at all; but if I think that according to the choices that are made, the kind of destiny of each one is determined, my faith in guardian angels remains even firmer.

Everything can be chosen in life since we are free, we have the right to decide what kind of work to do, in which city to live, who to meet, what kind of life we aim to achieve, no one can take away this faculty.

If we do not decide for our lives, it will be someone else who will do it for us, with the consequence of then living a life maneuvered by others.

Deciding is the highest expression of our freedom and conveys dignity to man. A man who cannot decide is a slave or mentally impaired, in the second case it is not his fault, in the first case if you are not a slave you are under a dictatorship. If you can't decide for example who to run the state where you live because they don't give you the chance to vote you're under dictatorship, you can also call it in other milder words, but in a democracy you give the floor to the people, in a dictatorship you don't, so draw your conclusions. Free men must be able to decide, period. Men who don't have the ability to decide aren't free even if they think they are, because actually someone else is deciding for them. In a declared dictatorship you know you are not free while in a fake democracy they make you believe you are free but then you cannot decide and even when they make you vote to make you think you are free then it will end and soon that someone else will command someone else, not chosen by the people, and they will take office and this is the biggest hoax. That is why, you should not believe under any circumstances that there is real freedom in all Western states.

Being free to choose also means being aware of the responsibilities that each choice entails: for example, you can decide to quit but then you have to be able to live with another job or find another one. Many individuals do not have the courage to make decisions and wait for others to do it for them, they are the ones who when they do something they say "I have" or "they have insisted that I have to", this is how their lives begin to be guided by other people. Think how nice it would be for these people to be able to say "I want", or "It's my intention", in this way they would have gratification or problems created only by themselves.

I think that with the same physical and mental conditions, the moment we are born we all have the same opportunities, therefore with the same chances of succeeding. There are those who think that in life only those who were born with a silver spoon in their mouths, those who win a prize pool or those who inherit a fortune, can succeed. These conditions can only help in part and only if accompanied by a set of qualities that allow the maintenance of a certain capital over time. I could cite stories of men born billionaires who after a short time squandered entire fortunes, or children of wealthy entrepreneurs accustomed to having anything and everything that a child would want, eventually ending their lives at a young age, destroyed by alcohol and drugs or committed suicide for their internal distress, because they had not been the maker of their own fortune.

Those who know the secret to their own success are aware that if they fall they know how to get up and may have the chance to do it again as they did the first time because they know what they have to do to build their fortune unless it was just a stroke of luck the first time. Then, to achieve true success, you have to have fallen many times before, to at least have the formula of lasting success. And then what satisfaction would there be in having something that you were not able to earn on your own?

History is full of incredible tales: there are so many men born out of nothing who have come to build businesses that they did not even dream of accomplishing.

"A matter of luck!" Some might say, but it is believing in luck that is precisely one of the fundamental causes of failure, believing in a blindfolded Goddess extinguishes trust in one's personal abilities.

I once heard that luck is for those who have the courage to go looking for it and that luckily there are skeptics because they will always come later.

The principles that inspired me most were basically these two: the first was to think that if others before me had made it, then I could very well have done it too, the second was to never take anything for granted for better or worse.

Why do many dissatisfied people complain about what they have, but do nothing really incisive to change? Simply because they don't think they can do it and they hide behind the false excuse of "I can't find anything else", "it's hard to change", "I was not born lucky". These excuses are true only in small part, the truth is the fear of going to meet the unknown and suffering. The fear of not making it, leaving behind the little that they possess even if it sucks, of not knowing if what they will meet will be better or worse than what they already have. Then it's better to stay inside their comfort zone. These fears are stronger than the desire to change and in order to change, first you have to face and overcome your fears and truly believe in yourself, preparing yourself as best you can. You can't believe in yourself if you know you're not prepared because inside you know you don't have the tools to be able to get by on your own and fight against everyone and win. If you are well prepared and feel strong, you know that you can win then go to war proud and demonstrate your strength. Fear and lack of desire to face change is reserved for the unprepared.

That is why I affirm that a man's greatest flaw is fear. Think of all those men who have accomplished extraordinary feats: every undertaking is born first in the mind, if at the time of conceiving it, they had taken for granted the fact that they might fail, today we could not all enjoy many exceptional works or for example fly by plane from one continent to another.

To build something that exists only in our minds until now, not having the certainty of succeeding in the enterprise, the only place to find the courage to start is within us. To find courage you always start from the idea that if someone else made it from scratch then you can do it too, because we are all on the same planet Earth.

If you do not believe in yourself and if you have no particular ambition then the only way to survive is under the wing of someone else, the state or a private enterprise.

A great entrepreneur said: if the road to success was already paved then everyone would go down it.

Who wouldn't want a beautiful house or a luxury car, for example, but how many are really willing to make the sacrifices it takes to get it?

At the beginning of my career I learned at my expense that you can achieve anything in life, you just have to be willing not to give up, to learn from mistakes to improve and thus achieve the goal.

Easier said than done but, on the other hand I think it is right that a good thing represents a prize and that therefore it is within reach only of those who deserve it, this is meritocracy. Beautiful things or rather the most luxurious, cannot be for everyone but for those who have the ability to reach them, otherwise you would have a world full of even more people who do not want to do anything and are not prepared to overcome their fears, a world of demotivated people because they know that they can have the beautiful and luxurious things in life regardless. It takes things that represent rewards to be achieved, rewards for all levels of success.

One piece of advice I can give is to start getting busy right away, from the exact moment when you find out what you really want to achieve: often you fail because you don't even know what you really want.

According to the principle of choice, one can decide to live in one of two ways: by imposing on the world or by letting the world impose itself on you.

I had chosen the first alternative, I had made the most difficult choice, but the most important thing for a man was up for grabs: to meet my destiny, to live my real life and not to settle for another life project that was not what I was born for.

Every man was born to fulfill a task, if he succeeds in this he will feel truly satisfied, in line with his life, he will feel to ready to live the life which he is destined to live, otherwise his life will be nothing more than getting by, with a sense of perennial emptiness inside.

That day at Golden Shoes I said, "No I can't stay!" and began a new important phase of my life that after many years brought me here.

CHAPTER TWO

The next time you're tempted to brag,
dip your hand in a bucket full of water
and when you remove it, the hole left in the water
will give you the right measure of your importance.

(Og Mandino)

My name is James Jaspersen I am sixty-six years old and I am an Italian-American although my name is not very Italian.

Right now I'm sitting in front of a computer in the middle of the night, and I've decided to write a kind of short biography, because I feel like I have to leave something written to someone, because maybe more than one person will read this book.

I'm going back in time to bring to light facts and the people who have allowed me to get here, this is a very intimate moment, I would also say magical, I hope that the vibrations of this moment can be felt through these words.

I have never met my real parents but through searching for my true origins I have come to know enough to understand how and why I am in the world. I was raised by two good people, my adoptive parents: Smilla and Santino.

My mother Smilla did not have a stable job, it was Santino who carried on the shack with a night patrol job. We lived in a modest suburb, one of those neighborhoods where walls are littered with anti-police graffiti and where kids meet at the bar talking about everything and nothing.

It's been 18 years since I was last in my old neighborhood. It would have been better to remember it as it was, it was sad to show my daughter Jasmeen that the place where her father grew up is a conglomerate of modern buildings home to companies and large franchised dental practices.

I had a strange feeling, as if they had stolen a piece of my life; I wanted to see the palace that I had lived in for many years, where I played football, the streets where I used to ride my bike, but nothing; everything had changed and seeing all this gave me a hint of bitter melancholy.

I remembered the faces of people who are now dead, naively I thought I could see them there somewhere maybe aged but still there. I still remember them young and it does not seem like reality, that they are almost all dead. As it also does not seem real to me that I am no longer a boy, and that now I am older than the people who died younger than the age I am now, people who called me a kid. If I close my eyes to remember the years of my youth, the first thing that comes to mind is the strong hatred I had for school. The imposition of certain rules and certain literature made me consider all books as boring and useless. I did not understand how texts that included outdated terms and dealt with issues that we young people did not identify with could be important to a man's life.

Years later I realized that it was the wrong way of teaching, the professors set themselves up by imposing themselves without explaining how certain subjects such as history, grammar, geography or mathematics can better help a person's future life. I understood it after school while working because without knowing the basics of mathematics you can't do the economics and your accounts well, you end up wasting a lot of money. Without geography you don't understand where you are and from what context many people you meet come from. Without grammar you cannot express yourself well and appear ignorant.

Without history you cannot understand the present and future because you would make the same mistakes that many people have made many years before you, and knowing history when you travel you can understand many more things about the places you visit. But at that time I didn't know this, I thought it was just useless things. I hated any kind of book, so much so that I swore to myself that as soon as I graduated, I would no longer open one, but today I have managed to do many things that I would not have believed achievable, because I did not live up to that promise.

I do not want to take credit for the work of great writers and poets such as Manzoni, Leopardi or Foscolo, but I believe that one of the fundamental reasons why many people after school have lost interest in reading, is due to the bad memories from their school years.

Forced to study nineteenth-century novels that do not have any relevance to our current reality.

Another cause of my loss of interest in studying was seeing some of my classmates considered "role model students", just because they knew how to shut up and stay still during classes, because they were intimidated by the reaction of their parents to a bad grade, and they memorized the pages of a book without understanding the true meaning. I was convinced that one day, life would fail them, because outside it's not about pretending to be good, you really have to be good to succeed. Unfortunately for many of them I was right.

My teachers thought that belittling those who got something wrong might be the right way to make them better.

I still remember certain phrases that were said to me: "James Jaspersen, you won't have a good future out there!" Or "you'll be a failure!", "look for a manual job, you don't have the head to do anything else! Listen carefully to these words because they will accompany you all your life." That was the perception most of my teachers had of me. They were right about one thing: those words accompanied many years of my life as a stimulus to prove otherwise.

I wonder what they would say if they saw me now sitting in this armchair, behind the desk of this office overlooking from the top floor of this skyscraper in a metropolis that many call "The Big Apple".

It's a great night right now here in New York, if I turn to the window and look out, the stillness I see makes me forget the chaos and the millions of cars and taxis that I see on it every day.

It's enchanting to see the huge nightscape of dark skyscrapers dotted with a few lights still on, this still makes me as ecstatic as the first time I landed here.

At the age of sixteen I had found a summer job that allowed me to spend the whole summer in a holiday village in Sardinia as a caddy. Caddy means being the golfer's clubs holder, you have to do the whole game with him, bringing him clubs for hours and even going to pick up the balls.

They played about three games a day, the first one started in the morning at 7:30 and each lasted about five hours. I had to walk for miles up those green lawns, attending the player I was assigned to. In that village I started to mature and get to know myself. I was younger than the rest of the staff, so if I wanted even a little consideration I had to prove to be worth at least as much as the others who were older than me. There I understood for the first time that if you want to reach important goals quickly you have to continuously put up with people who are more experienced than you and learn lessons that come out of that competition. If you lose after competing with a more experienced person, you have still learned something. If you compete against a person with less experience than you and still win, you have learned nothing.

There is an ancient saying that sounds like this: "The view of a dwarf is limited because of its height, compared to that of a giant that has a larger one. But if a dwarf climbs on the shoulders of a giant, it sees even further than the giant."

I returned to Sardinia to work in the summer also the years to follow and every time I returned home and enthusiastically told friends about the things that had happened to me, I was disappointed to see their disbelief and with time I became a man of few words. You can't compare yourself to those who have been left one step behind, they can never understand you all the way and a lot of people also have a sense of envy, and then try to downplay the things you've done better or more than them, out of the frustration of being left behind.

At the end of the season, once home, I had to once again face the usual real everyday life that I had forgotten about in the holiday village. That of the holiday village was not real life, it was like living in a golden microcosm.

At first when I came back, the first few days I had no desire to readjust, also because I did not like everyday life before, let alone after I had experienced the life in the holiday village, the comparison was even worse, and I could not accept the fact that I had returned to a monotonous life. Everyone told me I had to resign myself to the fact that that was the real life everyone has, but I didn't want to believe that this was the only way to live. I needed stimuli, to win or lose, to try to do something extraordinary, to accept challenges that made me feel alive, I wanted to live not only exist. At eighteen years old after two years of summer seasons in that holiday village I set myself a goal: I would return to a holiday village but only as a customer, I wanted to be served and not to be a servant, this also applies to my life.

I finally had a goal but I did not know what to do to achieve it. When I was coming up with an idea and discussed it with a few friends, if it was something modest I was supported, while if it was big ambitious projects, I was getting used to hearing myself repeating to let it go. They told me real life is another thing and that only few succeed in achieving big goals, and I wasn't one of them. Fortunately, however, by character I have always distrusted all those people who live a life by hearsay. Those who have never faced anything on the front line, fearing failure or suffering. How does a person give you advice on something they've never done before? If you have to accept suggestions about a matter, take them from an industry expert who really shows you that they know that topic well, otherwise everyone would be an expert in this life. There are people that before starting a new enterprise, let someone else go first, someone who will act as a lab rat, and then based on their success or failure they decide whether to try or not.

They are those who hide behind a mask of falsehoods from which they negatively judge those who, as opposed to them, have tried everything on their own skin before knowing what is right or wrong.

A mistake always hides a great lesson even if in that moment we are blinded by the sacrifice to pay and seems to us like everything is a misfortune. It was in the difficult moments that I was able to completely turn the situation around even more than I expected. In those moments the brain works faster and has to hurry to find a solution to lift us up. This is how solutions are often found that, in addition to putting us back in shape, can take us back beyond the break-even point. Having understood this, every time I tried to get something new and better out of my life. I would purposely put myself in a difficult situation to see how far I could reach and how I would turn the situation around, it is the way I grew up.

When I was nineteen, I left for military service, which was still compulsory at the time, when I returned a year later with no clear idea of my future, I bought a ticket to London.

It was the first time in my life that I had ever been abroad, I arrived in London at eleven o'clock in the evening at Gatwick Airport, with two suitcases, a few pounds, the hope of finding a job and in my pocket the address of a small budget hotel where I would spend the first night.

As soon as I left the tube, I noticed four guys smiling strangely at me, they were dressed in black, their faces made up of white, and after confabulating with each other they started following me. My mood at the time was not the best because I did not speak English very well yet, but I still tried not to lose my composure. I knew that if all of a sudden I started running for sure their reaction would be to chase me, so I stopped by a lamppost waiting for their first reaction.

A few seconds later the four of them approached me and told me something that I didn't understand very well with my English at the time, but then one word immediately made me understand what it really was. It was the thirty-first of October and it was Halloween, at that time in Italy no one knew what Halloween was, it was not celebrated, someone after watching an American film might have seen it but did not know what it was. After the four boys realized that they were not dealing with an Englishman and that I had not understood anything they let me go. I still remember with tenderness that moment because I realized how different times are now, that Italy has been celebrating Halloween for many years.

Seeing London for the first time was an indescribable emotion, an emotion that I will never forget. It was the realization of a dream, also because London has always been the dream of many people around the world. It is considered one of the most important cities and for me as for many others even now, a magical place. The thing that surprised me was that somehow I felt like being at home, as if that city had long belonged to me for long time. London was different at that time, the skyline back then was very different, there were no skyscrapers that exist today, many other important areas of today such as Canary Wharf, Stratford or the whole area of the O2 for example did not exist, I cannot even say what was in those areas because you didn't see anything until the underground took you there and I don't think there was any reason to. Some underground and overground lines did not exist, everything rotated mostly close to the center in zone one and two. Zone three seemed to go to the suburbs. Even the food at that time in London was different, there were no franchise chains of the various Cafés that exist today, or the chains of Pret a Manger, the kitchen was not like today where you eat well in many places regardless of the type of cuisine. At that time there was much less choice and the prices were even higher, in fact I could only afford two or three sandwiches a day.

London is a melting pot of different cultures that welcomes everyone and makes you feel at home, giving everyone the same opportunities and it is up to you to exploit them and if you prove to be valid and you want to do something you can go a long way.

The small hotel where I slept the first night was located near the Earl's Court Underground station, it was called the Royal House Hotel but it was actually a one-star establishment with shared bathroom. The next day I bought a travel pass for the underground which allowed me to move around in zone one and zone two, I was so glad to be there that I couldn't stay more than an hour in the same place. I didn't have any destination in particular, I wanted to see everything and right away, I was very satisfied with myself because staying there was the result of the money I had set aside by bringing people golf clubs a whole summer before leaving for the military.

It was a very different world from the small town in which I was used to living in, a huge metropolis that looked down on me and I in front of all that greatness felt insignificant and even very lonely. That's because it's true that London welcomes everyone but then you have to get by on your own. London provides you with opportunities, but then it's like a battlefield: everyday people go to war to earn their small or big space and if you want to be considered you have to be good at making room. Another thing that struck me was to see the respect and love for the music that the English have, in every underground station in shifts every day you can see different musicians, they come one after another in the same space and you can hear live music constantly. In some Underground stations there was a piano that anyone could play for free, this makes you understand how they respect music, how important it is for them. It is no coincidence the greatest songwriters and modern musicians are all English. In Italy in addition to not having regulations for street musicians on the street, they are despised, as If playing music on the streets was just about being a beggar.

During the day there is no time to stop to talk, you have to run to work and move from one side to the other to try to get there on time. People just stop at the end of the day to have a chat holding a beer but if you really want to talk to someone local you have to speak English well like them and that's why you were either born there or it takes years of learning.

I left with little money with the hope of finding a job immediately, in such a way that I would start to earn and support myself with the money earned there, but unfortunately I ran out of money shortly after finding the first job, because the first paycheck would be given to me after two weeks and I, not knowing how to survive for two weeks without money, reluctantly decided not to accept the job and return to Italy.

I left the English capital with a lump in my throat and a lot of anger at not having made it and I promised myself that it was not over for me there: one day I would return in very different conditions.

When I got home, I was surprised to find a job, he had vacated a job as an employee at the night patrol command office where Santino worked and had spoken to his commander to try to get me that job.

Santino was very happy to have found me that place and told me that I had to consider myself lucky to have found,at my age, a permanent place for life, at least so he thought.

I started stamping the card a week later but that only lasted two weeks, I felt like a useless person who was wasting his life doing things he never dreamed of doing.

"But what's the point of my life if I'm going to spend it locked up in here in this office checking data and invoices," I thought,

"Where will I see the world? One week a year if I can save money to travel? And if I'm worth something, how can I prove it to myself and then to others? How do I prove it locked in here every day doing the same job for someone?", was all I thought about every day from the moment I walked in until the moment I left that place.

When I decided to quit working with Santino, he felt very bad, he believed that I would become a failure, that I would never do anything in life. "Do you know how many guys your age are looking for such a place and don't find it? Now that place will be assigned to someone else and you will never find a job like this again! You will regret it all your life, you will see! I can't do anything for you anymore!" These were some of the things he said to me when I quit. From that moment on, our relationship was no longer the same.

I could also understand it, he was a simple man and with his mindset he could not conceive a person who would leave a permanent job called "safe" without having a valid alternative. He was one of those who did not believe in dreams, he did not believe that dreams can also be realized, he believed that if you are born into a rich family only then you can live a wealthy life, but if you are born into a modest family, you are destined to scrape by.

Although I quit without having any alternative, I felt I did the right thing, I felt like a bird who has fled its cage, I felt free again. Furthermore I considered the fact that If I continued, after few years they might decide to fire me, and starting from scratch would be even more traumatic.

In any way I looked at it, I've dodged a threat, but now I had to think about not becoming a failure, as Santino said.

I didn't sit with my head in my hands, I bought the newspaper full of ads in search of a job that I might be interested in.

CHAPTER THREE

*Your second life begins when
you realize you only have one.*

As I was trying to find a job, there was a phone call for me, it was Angelino, a childhood friend I often saw who asked me what my plans were for the future.

My intentions were clear: if I didn't find an interesting job I would leave for the United States or Australia, to start a new life there. I had nothing to lose and that made me strong and free to do anything. I just needed to set aside some money to be able to leave.

He asked me to accompany him to a job interview, it was a salesman's job at an advertising agency. So to do my friend a favor, I agreed to accompany him.

When they saw me at the interview they thought I was there to apply for the job as well, so they offered to hire me, but it was actually only Angelino's insistence that convinced me. What we liked about that job was the fact that they told us that we could spend the day as we wanted, or at least so we thought. All that mattered was the result and every month we had a budget to reach through sales., it meant that if we reached the budget in a single week then the rest of the month we could do nothing.

There was a sense of freedom that came with it and the idea of being able to earn a lot of money without having constraints pleased us very much and we believed that in the end it should not be too difficult to achieve. Shortly after we started, however, we discovered that the reality of a salesman's work was very different to how it appears.

At the time I had an old dark BMW 518, I had paid very little for it but a month later I understood the reason for that price when I had to fork out almost double the purchase price in repairs.

So I had to make money in order to keep up with the monthly cost of the laborious repairs that had become like a fixed installment.

A month after starting that job as a salesman and not seeing results but mostly many "no thanks", I realized that that job was not for me.

As soon as I showed up at a company taking my briefcase, they looked at me like I was a robber and the many nos I had received every day made me change my mind more and more about that job.

"Good morning I'm James Jaspersen, I'm from ..." "come again later because I don't have time to listen to you now!"

"Listen, if I had to listen to everyone like you that spends every day trying to sell me something then I wouldn't even have time to work, go away!"

"We don't need anything thanks!" "The owner is in a meeting!"

"Sales agents are only seen on Wednesday afternoons!"

"Thank you, but I already have my suppliers and I don't want to change!"

These were the main negative responses and I can assure you that it is not nice to hear them said all day long.

These answers made me envious of my friends who had found a safe jobs and those who had enrolled at University.

Those who worked as employees did their eight hours; they came home without any more thoughts and at the end of the month they got a fixed salary; those who studied went to the University in the morning and in the afternoon after studying they had free time, and in comparison to me both those who worked and those who studied were much more carefree.

I divided my friends into five categories: those who had found work as employees or workers; those who had gone to work in their father's company; those who had decided to study with the clear aim of doing a certain profession; those who did not know what to do had enrolled in the University under the guise of studying; and those who didn't want to study or pretend, or look for a job and lived without doing anything with their parents and occasionally doing little jobs.

A man like me was included in the fifth category, because the seller's job until you started to show concrete results is wrongly considered a fallback job.

Despite not liking that job, I did not want to prove those who thought that I was just wasting time right because I did not want to go and find a so-called "real" job. I did not want to resign myself to a job as an employee that I didn't like, so I kept going and after three months I looked for another company to represent. These were months when the succession of companies I changed trying to find the right one, were no longer counted. After a little more than a year I had resigned myself: I had come to the conclusion that it was no longer appropriate to keep trying.

I liked that sense of freedom and autonomy that being a salesman gave me, but I no longer knew how to pay for gasoline, car repairs and all the other expenses, I had accumulated only debts and also I had lost all the motivation it takes to do this job. It was going really badly for me even though the decline had not yet arrived I saw that it was really close, but I could not afford the luxury of standing with my head in my hands waiting to sink completely.

I came up with the idea of leaving for the United States where I would start a new life from scratch, but I lacked enough money to leave, and maybe even courage. Thinking and thinking of a solution, all of a sudden I had a lightbulb moment, I don't know if that is the right thing to call the so called mysterious help that I received but, now I am sure it was not luck.

More than once I have had proof that we are helped by one or more presences, in my opinion giving a natural explanation to everything that happens to us does not help us understand the true meaning of our existence. Believing only what we see doesn't really help us understand.

I do not mean to say that believing in a higher being helps to live better only because it gives comfort and makes us feel protected; there are many things that we do not understand and that we do not know, inexplicable events have happened to everyone, I believe in the presence of a guiding spirit that is always close to us and that I am never entirely alone. What I thought of doing was finding another job, which could allow me to set aside some money to go to London or America to start a new future. I was disappointed with Italy, the bureaucratic system, the absurd taxes and the narrow Italian mentality.

In my town there was a big shoe factory that I saw every day along my way home, something whispered to me that was where I had to turn to look for another job even though I hadn't seen any ads anywhere. So one sultry August day, driven only by the desire to make some money to be able to leave Italy I found within me the last shred of enthusiasm to phone Golden Shoes.

CHAPTER FOUR

*"There is a time in life
when what we dream
becomes what we do."*

(Arturo Mazzeo)

The August air at that time was unbearable and it was even more asphyxiating inside my old black BMW, an air-conditioned car at that time seemed to me like an unattainable wish.

I was desperate, I didn't want to stay in Italy anymore and I was just looking for a way to make some money to be able to leave, I knew very well that any word of this in a job interview could not slip out, otherwise no one would hire me.

I had to play the part of the humble boy, willing to work and learn. In that context of mental confusion and despair, one morning I dialed Golden Shoes phone number. An extremely sensual female voice answered me, so sensual that I was immediately tempted to ask if I had phoned an erotic line. After requesting a job interview, the secretary asked me if I would be so courteous as to wait in line, while she asked the personnel manager.

When the 'waiting' music ended, I heard her voice when offering me an interview for the next day at three o'clock in the afternoon directly with the sales manager.

The next day at the appointed time I found myself on time, ringing the bell of Golden Shoes.

Long hair kneaded with gel, Elvis Presley-style sideburns, left lobe earring, tieless white shirt, blue jacket, jeans and suede shoes without socks, this was my look that day.

I did not know yet that in certain circumstances that the suit helps to make the man.

As soon as I showed up at the lobby, the sensual voice that had answered me on the phone showed her face, begged me to sit in the waiting room because Mr. Feret would receive me shortly.

There was a circular table, chairs and newspapers in the waiting room, but what struck me was a phrase framed on the wall that said:

IF YOU WANT TO BE HAPPY FOR AN HOUR

TAKE A NAP

IF YOU WANT TO BE HAPPY FOR A DAY

GO FISHING

IF YOU WANT TO BE HAPPY FOR A YEAR

INHERIT A FORTUNE

IF YOU WANT TO BE HAPPY FOR LIFE

LOVE YOUR JOB

(HERAT'S ANSARI)

Soon after, the sensual-voiced secretary called me and accompanied me to the office of Alain Feret, the sales manager.

I was convinced that I would be facing a middle-aged gentleman, impeccably dressed in blue double-breasted suit with a serious look, but instead the one who was waiting for me was quite another person.

He was in his early thirties, well dressed but casually: a pair of blue cotton pants, a sky blue shirt with slightly rolled up sleeves and a pair of brown loafers.

As I entered his office he tried to get comfortable, with his hand he beckoned me to sit, at that moment I could see a small red lily tattooed on his right wrist, a drawing that looked like a coat of arms of a noble family.

At that moment the first thing that came to mind was "I understood that I have again messed up!" and I also thought that there were only two alternatives: either that company did not have enough money to hire a "real" sales manager or that was one of the many aforementioned sons of dads.

So, on the inside I was hoping that that interview wouldn't last long so that I could go quickly to look for another interview. But his eyes showed something mysteriously different, they weren't particularly beautiful, nor did they have a strange cut, they looked like they were magically getting inside my head, you couldn't lie in front of him.

He began to ask me about my work experiences and why I had turned to them. I told him about my short career as a salesman, making myself look as good as I could possibly look with small successes.

He was staying still listening to me, so much so that sometimes I didn't understand if he was really listening to me or if by education he just pretended. After twenty minutes I had nothing else to tell him and I was embarrassed because he didn't immediately start talking, he stayed quiet for a few seconds to look at me before saying, "James are you still convinced you're a salesman? I mean, are you still convinced that this is really the right job for you?"

It blew me away! But how did I just spend twenty minutes telling him about all the companies I had worked for, all while embellishing the stories of all the beautiful things I had encountered, just for him to turn around and ask me that question? That's when I realized that all the lies I had told him had been discovered and I started sweating.

I tried to get calm down because I thought that if I could get through that interview and get myself hired I could stay there for three months which is just enough time to set aside some money to get out of Italy. So there was a different future up for grabs, away from Italy and that could be my chance to earn it.

When asked if I was still convinced that I was a salesman, I replied with a firm belief: "Of course I am!"

So he looked at me and said, "I'm asking you this question because you're very young and it's often that at the beginning you're in this profession because you don't know what to do with your life or because you think you're earning so much money right away. There are also those who initially do it as a momentary job while waiting for some bank or public entity to which they have previously applied to, to call them. Why do you want to continue to do this profession?"

Another few seconds of awkward silence and embarrassment followed, because I didn't really want to keep being a salesman.

After thinking about the best answer I said to him: "I would like to do a job where I can be truly appreciated for what I'm worth. I'd like to see how far I can go. I want to have the freedom to take action. One day I want to be able to afford the house and the car I really want. I'm trying my best to make my dreams come true, and if I fail, at least I can say I tried. I think I'm worth it and I want to find out if I really am!" After a few seconds of silence, he looked me square in the eye and gave a deep sigh and said, "Congratulations James! I must say that it is not easy to see so much determination and clarity in a boy of your age. Surely so far you haven't had much from life or even the right opportunity to come forward, but I'm glad to see you're looking for your way. Tell me the truth, how many times have you thought about quitting, giving up everything and changing your life?"

That's exactly what I felt at that moment, in fact I was sincere and replied, "Well... really until today I've had this idea in mind"

He smiled at me and said, "There are still many more times when you will feel like giving up, until you have reached a certain position, you can believe me on that! Many will try to discourage you, to put sticks in your wheels. These will be hidden tests but every time you pass them you will unknowingly find yourself nearer to the destination. Every time something goes wrong, it's the way you react that will determine your fate. A defeat today can be a victory tomorrow, because by making mistakes today you will learn lessons that will make you win in the future. Not everyone achieves what they set out to do, they stop just before they are about to take one more step towards finally grabbing what they had been chasing for years. Doesn't that sound bizarre to you? It happens because they don't know it at that moment. It's like when you've been hitting for years on a woman who doesn't want to know anything about you and just when you decide to let go she falls in love with you but doesn't tell you. From the way I've heard you talk, it seems like one of the things you want the most is to get rich, is that it?"

He had just met me, but he already understood many things about me. "Well... yes, that's something I can't deny," I replied.

"What fascinates you about money?", he asked.

"I think money can improve the quality of life and especially give you freedom and peace," I replied shyly

"Do you think money can give you happiness?" he asked me.

"Very often yes! I don't think there are many happy poor people out there" I replied.

"A security related only to money generates anxiety, because one lives with the fear of going back being poor or becoming one, so some rich people make up for it with greed. Money will never fill a sense of inferiority if you have it. Have you ever seen those who flaunt their riches through some luxury goods and behaving a certain way? Don't you think if these people were really sure of themselves they wouldn't need to flaunt so much? By this I do not mean that those who buy a certain type of cars want, at all costs, to show off. I do not want to fall into the mistake of generalizing".

"I also want to earn a lot of money to prove to myself that like others that have succeeded before me I can do it too, I don't think I'm any less!" I said.

"Don't get me wrong, I'm not saying that this ambition is negative, but it depends on the spirit with which you deal with it. If you work for the sole purpose of making money, you can also become rich, but you will be impoverished inside. If when you make some money you do not want to live with the anxiety of losing it, you have to be aware of your abilities to understand that the money you managed to make is not the result of randomness and luck but of your skills and this must force you to understand that if you lose it you can make it again as you did the first time and thinking about this can give you more serenity".

He told me things no one had ever told me before and it really hit me a lot.

"I've decided to help you! Are you ready to start an adventure that will never end? Because if you really are what you say you are for you there will never be retirement for you. Retirement exists for those who work, not for those who make their work a tool to carry out their projects and make their work a way of life. You will live many moments of solitude, because those who want to emerge are not always understood, those who want to emerge attract envy even of some loved ones and friends who instead of supporting them will leave them. You must be ready to endure the loneliness, the so-called solitude of the number ones. You will know many moments of discouragement because very often things will not go as you think you deserve. Many moments of fear in which to give in to a quieter life and another safer job would be very easy. I hope you will have a woman next to you who will support you, because having a woman who supports you even morally will be important because you will need it. After all, you are a man and as such you are not invincible, remember it! When you go through those moments imagine you are a warrior and you are wearing an armor resistant to everything, the strongest there is, nothing and no one can bring you down and can prevent you from reaching your goal. Convince yourself that you are the strongest, so others will believe it too. I will stand by you, I will teach you how to fight, but one day when you have learned you will have to get by on your own and you will be protected by the teachings I will give you if you put them into practice. Now I ask you, are you really determined to start this great challenge?" he concluded, looking me in the eye.

I looked at him and said "ready! When do we start?" We had just met but it was enough for him to understand me, for years I needed to hear someone say to me those words. I terribly needed someone to force me to do what I knew how to do.

From that moment I had become like a piece of marble in the hands of a sculptor, the artist when he creates does nothing but cut away at the marble with the chisel, the shape is already inside.

Now that so many years have passed and everything has happened, I remember with melancholy and nostalgia those afternoons spent in his office listening, learning, and even though for many I have become a teacher today, I also need a master.

I miss his reproaches, his encouragements, his silences and even the moments when I hated him because he was too harsh with me and I didn't believe I deserve it.

"We'll start by setting a method, we'll come up with an action plan, the first thing is to have a goal in mind. You'll need to know day by day what you need to do and why. Without proper organization, you cannot really get anywhere; you would be like a boat at the mercy of the sea, you would waste so much useful energy without getting results. The first important thing you'll have to learn to do is to be able to distinguish important things from urgent things. Many people do urgent things first, thinking they are also important things but often they are not and leave out what is really important. In this way they end up doing so many things producing few results not knowing why."

Before I left his office he took a piece of paper, took out a pen, wrote a few lines, folded it in two, and handed it to me.

He said, "Read it only before you fall asleep! I wish it would stick in your mind. You know what one of the things I appreciated about you was? It was the fact that you showed up here without thinking about whether or not we were looking for a person, you were resourceful. This is a spirit of initiative and is one of the skills you will need to go far. Never wait for things to happen to you, make them happen!"

Just outside I was dying to open that folded piece of paper but I wanted to respect his recommendation to open it before I fell asleep, so that night I went to bed early to read it.

The note read this:

Every obstacle is a bridge

Like a big stone in the middle of the river

It may be an impediment

If we stumble against it

And if we pretend to take it off

But it can help

To switch between shores

If we walk on it

In this case

The bigger the rock

The easier crossing to the other side will be

But the rock itself is just a rock

It's up to us to see it as an obstacle

Or use it as an opportunity.

Five minutes before I met him, I was just thinking about making a bunch of money so I could get out of here and go to America, an hour after I met him, I knew that had just found my America.

That was the day that changed the course of my whole life and nothing would ever be the same for me.

CHAPTER FIVE

"Everyone in life needs a mentor"

(Arturo Mazzeo)

The next day I showed up in Alain's office, an office where his imprint was clearly evident: a small cactus above a white cabinet where inside there were about thirty motivational books stored in height order, a map of Italy hanging on the wall with some small colored flags, a black desk where a series of documents were placed neatly.

There was no difference between his armchair and the other two front posts, they were all of the same pattern, color and height because Alain did not want those who went to see him to feel unconsciously subordinate to him.

That first morning he told me about the general trend of the company and then he personally accompanied me to show me the whole factory. I was fascinated to see how a shoe is created from scratch, the handmade seams and stitches, the small nails that were still being hammered in by hand, the small artisanal finishes that conferred value and characterized the real made in Italy product famous all over the world.

When I asked him why he had a French name I offered him the

excuse to tell me his story briefly.

His family was descended from an ancient and noble house of Provence, in fact the red lily he had tattooed on his wrist was his coat of arms. His parents separated when his mother learned of her husband cheating on her, but his mistress was expecting a child. After the divorce, the father moved with little Alain to neighboring Italy with the idea of starting a family with the American girl that made him divorce his wife and that was going to give him another child.

They went to live in Imperia but could not carry out that plan because his new partner died a few months after giving birth. That circumstance caused him to fall into a state of depression and he did not feel like bringing up a child alone without a woman by his side. The newborn ended up in an orphanage and shortly after was entrusted to a couple who could not have children. Alain had not had a good relationship with his father, he had not been very present in his life. He was more engaged in the trade of precious stones than in his upbringing. One day, after he had yet another argument with his father, Alain slammed the front door and told him he would never return and from that moment he started being a salesman. At that time, however, he had not considered that to start an independent life he had chosen one of the most difficult professions. He became good in a short time because he was moved by a strong economic need and pride, it is the need that gives you the necessary motivation.

For this reason, by the time he was thirty he was running one of the most important shoe factories in Italy.

When I made him realize one day that I still had insecurities and that I wasn't really convinced I could do it, he gave me this answer: "If you're convinced you can't do it then you're going to fail! If you're convinced that you'll succeed then you're going to make it. What you are truly convinced of, will come true. You will never be able to convince anyone if you are not convinced yourself first, because you will pass what you really think on to others and even your words will be different. You'll only get what you think you deserve. Never forget it! Remember this Indian saying: aim for the moon, if you miss at least you will hit the hawk but if you only aim at the hawk and you will miss, you will only hit the branch of a tree."

The first day of work did not last a long time, after visiting the factory he made me go home and told me that we would start working the next day.

The next day, knowing that I was going to start working, I wore the most elegant clothes I had and showed up to his office, proudly holding my leather briefcase, convinced that I would fill it with catalogues and price lists.

As soon as he saw me, he greeted me with a mocking smile, saying, "Why are you dressed like that?".

"Considering that I'm starting work today, I dressed as best I could to introduce myself to the first customers!" I replied.

"It's true..." he said, "Today you start working but on yourself!",

"How would I do that?" I asked in amazement.

"I mean, if you really want to build a safe future, you have to build a solid foundation first, just so in difficult times you'll be able to get up without waiting for someone's hand to pull you up! Because you never have to rely on anyone's help but only on yourself and to do that you have to be very prepared," he told me.

"And how can I build these solid foundations?" I asked him.

He turned to the cabinet where he kept his books and after taking one he said, "Starting with this!" He gave me a book, one of those things that I had hated for so many years at school, so I looked at him with mistrust.

"This is a book but you can also consider it a brick, not only because if you throw it at someone's head it will hurt, but because it is the first brick in your knowledge library. If you don't understand what I'm telling you now, don't worry, you'll soon understand. If you were going to visit the first customers today, if you could sell something, you could earn the first commission, but that would only help you to raise a few extra bucks, you would always stay who you are, without any personal growth. I'm sure that's not what you really want, is that what you want? Although, rightly so, you also need to earn something to make you feel comfortable I will pay you the same for as long as you stay here to study. But remember that I'm not a professor, you don't have to memorize anything, I won't question you, life will do it for me when you start leaving this office. These books are tools that serve to make you a better, stronger and more prepared person, use them well. I'll give you only one piece of advice: assimilate the concepts you read, make them your own and try to understand them to the fullest."

I couldn't believe that a commercial director of a company would talk to me like that, the same way you would talk to a child, or someone you love, another in his place would say to me: "Take... this is the price list, this is the sample, this is your area, now you can go and I recommend trying to bring back as many orders as possible!".

Then he said to me again: "One day if you haven't already asked yourself now, you'll wonder what I earn keeping a salesman locked in an office reading books. Someone could take me for a fool, I know. I'll answer before you ask me. Money is in many cases a consequence of what you do, it's a fair reward. The more important it is, the bigger the reward. I am very grateful to life because I recognize that so far it has given me so much, much more than I thought. Every day before I go to sleep I thank God for the life I have and for what I'm doing. I also realized that since I have come here at my age, it is also to help improve the existence of other people. I feel indebted to life. You don't help someone just by giving them money because the money runs out, you would help them more if you teach them how to earn it.

I'm not rich but I live well, the real rich go around on private planes and I'm not at that level because maybe I don't care enough yet. But if one day I ran out of all the money I have and I need to look for a job, I would know what to do to start from scratch and I am convinced that I would rebuild a career and earn all the money I lost. That makes me feel comfortable. This is the most important thing you need to learn: finding the right key that allows you to open all the doors, the key to your success! And you can find this key by putting together the notions you find in so many books. Commercially speaking then, there is also another reason that drives me to make you read all these books. Companies are organizations of people living for profit as the only goal, I am convinced that the first thing you need to invest in is not in state-of-the-art machinery because everyone can buy them, but the first thing to invest in is the staff. Machines will never replace creatives and intuition, machines have no intelligence, they are just executors of orders, orders that come from human intelligence.

One day, developing countries will be able to manufacture products similar to ours, at a much lower price. But they can never copy our made in Italy style and creativity. The only thing they can never do is produce style and creativity first without copying what they already see in the market, so if you want to survive the price war, you have to aim to always be unique and innovative. This concept for me also applies to sales because it is the same as training. If one day in addition to being a better person, you will also be a salesman able to produce a turnover thanks to the hours spent learning, then the time and money I invested in you was well spent," he concluded.

From that moment on, I felt a great responsibility on me and asked him, "What if it doesn't?"

"You can't be sure that a company succeeds before you've even tried, the important thing is to be convinced of what you do and put all the effort and enthusiasm you need. If you were to disappoint me, I still know I did the right thing: I couldn't have done better," he said.

CHAPTER SIX

It doesn't matter what you
know, but what you can do.

(Arturo Mazzeo)

As soon as I saw all that slew of books waiting to be read, at first glance my arrogance made me immediately think that they would not ne able to teach me anything new.

The first day I thought of using a cheap trick I had learned at school: that of pretending to read by staring at a page for five minutes and then moving on to the next.

Thank God, however, my curiosity intervened and little by little I began to immerse myself in a new world.

How could a book interest me so much when for years I had not even been able to finish one?

It was the first time I was reading something different, exciting, apparently obvious in some ways but few times fully put into practice. One of the first books was "How to Win Friends and Influence People" by Dale Carnagie.

Those books were discussing the rules of life, that practice, that of everyday life, they told what I needed to know.

For three months my job was to read and memorize, and then put into practice when the right moment would come. I was doing some sort of mental training. Occasionally I asked Alain if the time when I could start my job as a salesman had finally come but every time he replied just to wait, and the more he told me so the more my desire increased.

Finally after three months the time came when I could start putting into practice what I had read.

When you are full with motivation you feel like the best, invincible, you believe you can open every door, but when disappointments overcome the expectations, then you go back being vulnerable and fearful.

There are self-help, motivational, sales courses, held by gurus that make you believe that once you get out of there, you'll be a new person and from that moment onwards you'll be a winner and will begin to make lots of money. It would be nice if it was true, since there are gurus of that kind able to gather more than a thousand people for a live class and if every single time they would succeed in creating new winners and new millionaires it would be just great. Unfortunately it's not like that, the vast majority comes out of there very motivated, believing that, from the next morning,- their lives would be different. Soon after they will begin facing the same everyday problems and they will not see that sudden transformation they were expecting, thanks to the techniques learnt in the course; and slowly they go back to their old selves, their same old lives. It is not enough attending a class or reading some books to turn your life over; you need to be systematic and keep on trying. It might seem easy but it's not It might seem easy to think of becoming consistent but it's the hardest thing to do, because there are too often situations that go wrong and giving up is easier than carrying on.

The truth is that no guru can change you, the only one who can is yourself. Don't put your all your belief in a guru, put it in yourself.

After taking a course it takes little to find out that everything they promised, you can actually get it only after you have poured liters of sweat into your work. Many begin the path to pursuit of their dreams, it takes little to motivate a person, just find his weak point and make him understand that you will be the person who can help him. But few are willing to sacrifice years of their lives for something they believe deeply, often supported only by themselves.

The difference between a winner and a loser lies in the questions that they both ask themselves. The loser when faced with an obstacle asks: "Why did this happen to me?" A winner instead focuses solely on the solution by asking: "What can I do to solve this problem?".

There is also another truth: not everyone really wants to win, there are also those who prefer to lose or not face the challenge at all because deep inside they do not feel up to managing all the responsibilities and concerns that a possible success can give. Then there are the undecided ones who do not know whether to sign up for the race to success and stand there thinking too much, to keep trying, they are the ones who always wait for the right moment, but do not know that in fact by doing so they have already decided: they have already decided to lose by not starting because those who do not start do not go anywhere, always staying where they are.

When you are young and ambitious you have the risk of being impatient, impatience is very dangerous because it basically means wanting everything right away, but unless you win a lottery this is not possible.

I immediately wanted to become someone, buy a house right

away, have a nice car and not being able to have all these things gave me a sense of dissatisfaction.

I could not be satisfied with the present and the small goals already achieved, I immediately wanted the long-term ones.

A house is born first from a brick, and brick after brick you also build a large building, it all starts from a first brick though. When I returned to the company after a day of work visiting customers, and looked at my first, small, orders I was happy and at the same time also dissatisfied because I wanted to get more and from more important customers. Alain praised me for being able to see the first bricks of my future home. On the contrary, however, I desired the house be ready and furnished right away.

When we met with Alain, the thing I liked the most was to talk, because with his calmness and his confidence he always knew how to find the right words and the solution to any apparent problem. He once said to me, "If you want to achieve results in life, you must first know what your fundamental value is for you, and you will live according to it. Success in life does not necessarily mean being able to make money but being able to live the kind of life that you set out to achieve. Not everyone can live in line with their values, but life is an ongoing challenge."

"It's true!" I thought. "The important thing is to be able to live according to your values and quality standards, this is the real success."

You don't feel good about yourself when you're in a situation that doesn't belong to you, like hanging out with people who are not for us, living a kind of life that doesn't feel like ours, or doing a job that doesn't satisfy us. If a person is in this condition, all he can do is roll up his sleeves to repaint his whole life.

A man lives on average seventy-five years.

If at the beginning of his life he had as many sheets of paper as there were days to live, there would be almost twenty-six thousand. If we kept all that paper in our hands and every day we took a piece of paper and burned it, you might know how many days would be left to live.

Think about how important each single sheet is, would you give even one away? Yet how many days do we spend doing nothing, days that no one can ever give us back, for this reason every day is invaluable. In light of this reasoning, would you sell even one of your blank sheets knowing that you would have one less day to live? If your answer is no then don't waste a day, live them all intensely.

If you woke up every day automatically thinking that a new sheet is starting to burn, I'm sure you would do anything not to have regrets. The problem is that if you take an unlimited number of sheets for granted, you lose sight of the right way to live, you should instead think that our days are not unlimited.

CHAPTER SEVEN

No one is more disgraced
than an old man who has nothing left
to prove that he lived but his age.

(Seneca)

"You used to dress pretty elegantly, but for the past three days I have seen you go to work dressed like you wore the first thing you found in your closet!" Alain told me one day after seeing me wandering around the Golden Shoes offices.

"It's true that I let myself go after seeing so many other sellers dressed very casually," I replied.

"But do you want to be like the others or do you want to stand out?" he replied, "what do you know about the goals of these other sellers? You know your goals and you only have to look at those, don't care about others and what they do in their lives. It's not just a matter of looks, but from that you can understand many things about a person and especially from the details of the look. We produce shoes here, but not common shoes, shoes for numbers one, shoes for those who want to stand out, whoever wears our shoes does not go unnoticed, wearing our shoes is like driving a luxury car, have to live up to what you sell. Always do what's right for you, don't be influenced by others. When I was your age I wanted to prove at all costs how much I was worth, the fact was that I did this challenge for my father because I had not yet found my inner balance. I was always angry with everything and everyone, I wanted to show my father how much I was worth. I didn't realize, however, that he already knew it even though he couldn't prove it to me. Remember, however, that the opinion of others is not decisive if you know how much you are worth! You should not wait for someone to give you a compliment or appreciation to feel good, you must be satisfied with yourself regardless of what others tell you. Don't wait for the consent of others to do whatever comes to mind, if you think something is right for you then do it! There is only one person who knows what is right or wrong for you, mirror it and you will see it! You must first get to know yourself to overcome the adversity you will face. You have to be like an adventurer participating in great races in the middle of forests and deserts, races that last weeks. Certainly these men in addition to knowing how to drive well also know how to repair the engine of their car because if it stops in the middle of the desert they cannot certainly go to a workshop or call a mechanic to help. So those who want to get the most out of themselves must first get to know themselves well. Know how you react in certain situations, what your aspirations, tastes and abilities really are and understand how far you can go. To get to know yourself, you have to have the courage to test yourself by facing different situations that you have never faced before.

The reason why very few know themselves well is because they have never really been alone, they have always called and had someone next to them in their time of need. Until a certain age it is normal to be with your parents but it is them, believing that they are doing thier best to protect us from certain situations, who do not help us understand what our value is. As soon as we are born then they inculcate their ideas: "you have to behave like this... don't do this kind of sport because you are not suited for it... you have to study this... this is the religion to follow.... try to do this kind of work... you have to try to become as I would like... try to marry this kind of woman... don't dress like that..." and over time they make us think like them because they somehow affect our lives. Actually, we're not what our parents would like us to be. For example, in your opinion do you think a Catholic or a Muslim child, would really think that about religion if it weren't for their parents? No! This proves that religions are an invention of man. If it were not so, it would be natural for any person born into the world to think of it in the same way, in the matter of religion. On the other hand, since there are so many religions, it means that not every religion could have been dictated by God because since God expresses himself in one way there should be only one religion, same for everyone, but this is my personal thought.

When we grow up we understand what we really want for ourselves and if that contradicts what our parents want, we feel a sense of guilt as if what we want is wrong. A person with a capital P is first and foremost a free being, free of thought and judgement and has an autonomous identity. Many people will never know their true identity, in fact it comes to a point that when they talk, you cannot differentiate them from their parents. Others have mental limitations imposed by society, the people they date or their spouse. Friends push us to think in the same way as them, and often we do not have the courage to say no for fear of being alone. Our partner can condition us to think the same way; the media conditions us by showing us their version of events often rigged by opinions of biased journalists, broadcasting biased news disguised as neutral truths, but actually often completely distant from reality. Often times, looking at certain news, it shows we want to give the impression that now the majority of people think in a certain way by also showing us paid actors, passed off as random people in a demonstration or giving us inflated numbers of participants in a protest very different from reality to condition us. In all this, the human being with its own different thoughts is canceled and if he tries to stand out from the crowd he is looked at as an abnormal person. According to those who secretly manage the mass media we should all adapt and homologate to the same thought because for those who rule it is convenient to have people who are not able to think, better to have people homologated as much as possible to a single thought, imposed by those who govern and shame those who try to oppose. They begin with disparaging campaigns, putting the opposition in a bad light often by affixing labels as "fascist" that even if one does not recognize himself in fascist ideals at all, he will be passed off as an enemy of the people. The power knows that it does not matter what you really are or think, it is enough to just publicly label you as "racist", "fascist", "mafia" even if you are not, even without evidence, and just because that politician or that prominent journalist said this there will always be a negative shadow over you, and whatever you say will not have the same strength anymore.

Today they make you believe that you are in democracy just because you believe that everyone has the right to express themselves, only that if you say something politically incorrect or if an alternative journalist brings to light power games that enrich the ruling political party at the expense of the population, then they label what that journalist says as fake news. Fake news exists, the ruling political power created the term, to have a negative definition to be affixed to those who oppose them, promulgating news different from those of main stream and to silence opponents by passing them off as promoters of fake news. Do you understand what a perverse game they have invented? Fake news exists and their existence is convenient to the "power", but not all what they want you believe is fake, actually is. A part of fake news is artfully created and supported by "the power" to keep the concept of fake news alive in the population, because people need to know that fake news exists. This is because the moment that an opponent publishes an alternative news story to unmask some hidden power agenda, or shed light on what is really happening to the government then the "power" lashes out at those who publish that news, defending themselves from those accusations by answering that that is fake news, via the pro-government journalists who are the ones you often see in the most important television channels, who are always asked about opinions of various kinds, and the more they are publicly seen, the more they gain authority. If you often see journalists on various TV shows talking about political topics or being used all the time as commentators, you get used to them and for you in the end what these characters say starts to matter. So for the "power" to use some of them to disprove certain news is a very effective strategy. Are you beginning to understand how the whole system works and why many people think in a certain way? A leader, in order to assert his ideas, goes against all the system, he is not afraid to be left alone, at first they tell him that a certain thing cannot be done just because no one before him has done it, when then he manages to achieve the results he is praised and some of the people who had put sticks in his wheels or denigrated him at the beginning, will then try to give themselves credit for helping him, also saying that they had always believed in him. But all this can only happen if he eventually manages to win and to show results, because until that, for everyone you will be a failure even if your intentions were good, what matters is only the final results not the good intentions.

In Italy there is the bad habit of staying in the family until you get married, for some even after the wedding nothing will change because their home will continue to be the one in which they have always lived in, with their parents. This mentality that for those who are not Italian see this as an absurdity, it makes people who live in this way look like eternal children. It's easy to continue having your mother cooking for you, having someone who helps you do the shopping and pay the bills, but that doesn't mean you're really grown up. An adult person must know how to cope on their own not to continue to depend on their parents, age is irrelevant to be an adult, you can say that you have grown up when you are able to completely get by on your own, otherwise you will always be an eternal child.

All these concepts had opened my mind, awakening things that I already knew inside me and giving me greater confirmation of what I already thought.

I still remember what he said to me once when I asked him what I needed to do to be successful: "Remember that all your income will come from the ability you will have to understand the needs of those you will meet or the audience of people you will have identified as your potential customer. If you understand what they need and provide them that, thus creating a service or a customized product, then you will succeed. Ignorance means presumption and when you believe you know it all, you regress because you stop learning. There is no point of arrival at where you are satisfied to know what you already know." So I asked him, "Why are there ignorant people who have made it big?"

"It depends what you mean by ignorant and how far they have gone. There may be ignorant people who have come to occupy managerial and powerful positions but mostly in public places, because they are recommended by a relative in politics. But if you see an ignorant man at the head of a major private company this can happen because he has delegated many responsibilities to very competent people who manage the company on his behalf and he maybe just takes the credit for it. But there is no entrepreneur who has made it on his own and with his own strength to a really important level who does not know how to deal with others. If you really want to leave a mark of your existence, then strike the hearts of the people you meet. You really only disappear when you have been forgotten because you have not given enough, but to disappear because of this you do not necessarily need to die. No one is more wretched than an old man who has nothing left to prove that he lived but his age, Seneca said. If you analyze the most important technological discoveries in history, you will find out that they were made by those who had the courage to make logical what previously seemed illogical. So start thinking illogically and don't be afraid if they criticize you for that. Albert Einstein said that the most important thing is to see something in a dream and then fight for it to become logical and achievable. St. Augustine said that faith is to believe in what we do not see. If man had not believed in something illogical, would he have ever thought that a piece of iron with wings could fly from one side of the globe to the other? Or that he could even get to the moon? You were telling me about ignorant people who have become successful or heads of companies, but have you wondered if the companies of these gentlemen today thrive or sail in bad waters? Because there are companies that at any moment suddenly close, even if for years they were profitable. True success is seen in time, dig deeper and do not necessarily believe what others would like you to believe. I had met an entrepreneur who did not treat his employees well on a human level and had also created a hierarchical scale of employees to whom he had taught that treating the subordinates with condescension was the best way to make everyone work without demanding anything more from him. That entrepreneur, however, had not considered that his employees before being workers were people, with the same needs as he had. The consequences of his behavior was the progressive self-layoff of most of his staff and as a result he began to make a bad name in the area which did not allow him to reintegrate the staff. That led to a difficult situation, having also accumulated delays in deliveries and as a result began to accumulate dissatisfied customers who stopped buying from him. The competition was strengthened by acquiring his customers and shortly after, that entrepreneur had to declare bankruptcy. Do you understand the consequences of bad behavior towards employees are and what it can lead to? At the foundation of every company there are no machines, there are people, only harmony between people can take a company far. So try first of all to become a valuable person and success will come along.

There is a saying: only those who are crazy enough to think that they can change the world really change it. Then, James, begin to believe in madness!"

That day had started with Alain asking me the reason for my change of look and from that he had given me a series of valuable lessons that served me throughout my life.

CHAPTER EIGHT

*Failure is just a harsh lesson
in teaching what not
to do afterwards.*

(Arturo Mazzeo)

Many great managers and entrepreneurs claim to sleep only a few hours per night: the anxiety, the desire to do and the many thoughts that afflict them are the cause. They make so many sacrifices to build a better life, a peaceful future in which they will enjoy all that they have managed to create. They work with the future in mind, with their thoughts fixed on the realization of their goals. They live in the present with their minds turned to the future, building something they will exploit tomorrow, as long as they are still alive. In all this they forget that the present is the only real thing. The past no longer exists and the future does not exist, there is only the present and that is what you have to live for. If you lose sight of this, living too far ahead, it will result in you never fully enjoying your days

How many times have you stopped to look at the landscape at sunset and think it's beautiful? How many times during a sunset were you distracted by work or were you busy with something or you were running to catch a train and you ended the day in a sad way thinking only about what you are supposed to be doing tomorrow. You have never enjoyed a single minute of the present.

At the beginning of my career, one day I was on a secluded, dark street, when I was fed up with living thinking only of a better tomorrow, I wondered if it still made sense to keep collecting refusals after refusals every day.

At that time I was twenty-five years old, and I wondered if all those sacrifices will one day lead to something. When you receive refusals one after another it is not easy to overcome this stress, but getting through those moments led me to have what I have today. I went through so many moments when the temptation to give up everything, to take refuge in another "safer" job was really strong, especially when I realized I was working just barely enough to pay my debts. Many years ago there were jobs that could be considered "safe", so-called employee or worker jobs in which you never thought they would ever fire you and as soon as they hired you with an indefinite contract at that time you thought you got bingo. Over the years, things began to change and those "safe" jobs also proved precarious even if you had that contract, because if a company goes into difficulty it is forced to lay off even permanent employees, so many had to reconsider calling this type of work as "safe". The only job left that was "safe" remained that of permanent civil servant, but it does not concern the majority of the population. I have always thought that the only safe job in life is yourself, if you want to have the opportunity to work your whole life until you retire you have to rely on your professional experience that must be continuous and always up to date and then you will always have the opportunity to work, and if you do not find a job in your country you can always look abroad but only if you have something to offer.

This is because this kind of company is safe for life and since you are aware of this you must always have a plan B in the drawer to exploit if you need it.

What always drove me to move forward was the desire to fulfill my desires, even with regard to certain material possessions to which I aspired to have, such as an increasingly expensive watch or the increasingly luxurious car. But also the desire to see who would win the bet that someone had placed on me, there were those who saw me as a loser and who as a winner, of course I wanted to make those who had bet on me win.

When I started to see the first successes, I also began to make other kinds of mistakes that I hadn't made before, because I thought that it was not possible to get to a point where you don't make mistakes anymore, you just change the kind of mistakes you make, but you always make mistakes. Sometimes I didn't admit I was wrong, blaming other people and that was the best way to make the same mistake again.

As soon as I became a successful salesman I was entrusted with the management of the entire area where the Golden Shoes was present in Italy, and then also the responsibility of all the new stores, until I became the most important person after Alain Feret. I really felt proud of me at that moment because I would not have believed that all this could have happened in just over four years. At some point, however, what I had was no longer enough, I wanted to become like Alain, I wanted to match him and one day, also overtake him. In my pursuit, however, I realized that my master is a point of reference: one that can never be matched, let alone overcome, a master will always remain so in your mind. Through chasing Alain's tail I managed to climb steps higher than my leg would have been able to climb, without his thrust I would not have been able to achieve those results in a short time, I was like a plane that goes faster because it is also being pushed by the wind.

The first secret to success is to have a good teacher, if you have not been lucky enough to meet one, surrounded yourself with motivational and successful books.

My life changed again when one day I was contacted by an executive at one of Europe's leading shoe factories, with branches around the world: the Munari high-class Shoe factory.

The meeting with Dr. Sbrenna took place one afternoon in the office of their commercial headquarters in the center of Milan.

"The reason for our meeting is simple we would like you to come and work with us. We need someone like you on our staff. I've heard a lot about you and a person capable of gaining such a reputation is the right one, in my eyes" began Dr. Sbrenna.

"What kind of assignment are you proposing to me? I could never compete with Golden Shoes. I am too attached, it is like a family to me!" I wanted to point out.

"You can see that you are still young James, in trade there are no emotional ties, if you want to get to the top you do not have to look at anyone's interests but your own, also look at the story of the two Dassler brothers, they split up due to disagreements and one founded Adidas and the other Puma, from then on they were enemies until death even though they were brothers, Alain didn't tell you?" Dr. Sbrenna replied.

"How do you know Alain?" I asked in amazement.

"I can't hide from you that we've been chasing him for years but he's a stubborn man he doesn't want to give in," he replied with a wry grimace. "I bet it's not about money, is it?" I asked him.

"We even offered him to write his price in the contract, but that didn't convince him either, at this point I don't think he cares much about money, I think he has other plans for his future."

"If I do agree to work for you, I'll only do it on the condition that I get to do something I've never done before and that I wouldn't be able to do if I stayed with the Golden Shoes," I replied.

"I can see you're a pupil of Alain, as you know we're a much bigger company, what would you do if you come to work for us?" he asked me. "I would like to take care of your foreign market! Golden Shoes has outlets abroad but I don't think that they would ever let me take care of that market since Alain takes care of it," I replied.

"Do you think you're up to it since you've never done that? For us, export makes up 60% of our turnover and we can't afford to have the wrong person managing it" he told me.

"I'm sure I can do it, I like challenges, especially with myself and also now I know Italy thoroughly and it begins to feel tight for me. Maybe I'm giving you the impression that I'm arrogant, but I'd prefer to let you know right away what my goals are." Said.

"I appreciate your outspokenness, I must say that you are an even more ambitious than I thought. I'll think about it and let you know as soon as possible, in any case it was a pleasure to have met you," Dr. Sbrenna replied.

I had aimed for something really important because deep down I had nothing to lose. If he had not accepted I would have kept my place, but if he had I would have moved to a new one, thus improving my current position and my professionalism in a more established company. I didn't feel guilty about Alain for going to that interview because the gratitude and esteem I felt towards him hadn't changed and it would never change, but in life you can never say never and especially in work. When you make a deal and you have nothing to lose you are in the best position because you have the peace of mind that you can start with the highest demands because you are not afraid that they might not be accepted.

I remember a negotiation I made years later in Australia to enter into a major trade agreement for my brand with two local retailers. They showed up with eleven lawyers in tow while I had gone there alone with one of my collaborators because I hadn't given much weight to the thing at the time. The lawyers wanted me to explain all the clauses of the contract I had previously sent and after all my explanations their lawyers shook their heads in a sense of disagreement towards the two possible business partners. They were doing everything they could to put me in awe and at a disadvantage so that I could give them further concessions. At one point, however, I told them in a firm and determined tone that I was no longer willing to negotiate further and that I would have preferred to have closed the deal with two other local retailers who were as interested as they were, I looked at my watch and told them that I had only thirty more minutes to spare. At that moment their attitude changed and shortly after the agreement was mutually signed. I had no other deal at stake other than them and at that time and I was selling almost nothing in the Australian market and they were the most important retailers in Australia. They had seen my shoe collection at the last show in New York a month earlier and already knowing that my brand in Europe was going strong they were convinced that bringing it to Australia would be a fair move and they wanted the exclusivity. I didn't realize the importance of that deal at the time, and I set my sales terms not caring if the deal failed. It was good for me and the following year the turnover in Australia thanks to that deal was fifteen million dollars which then increased in the following years.

Four days later, Dr. Sbrenna contacted me again, telling me that the entire board of directors of the Munari Shoemaker had approved my request: I would become a commercial manager of their foreign market with a 5-digit base starting salary plus a commission on all the new turnover I would be able to bring. From that moment I would be living Milan, near the headquarters of the shoe factory.

The next day I was waiting for the most difficult task: telling this to Alain.

I entered his office with a sorry expression, I hadn't even started to speak when he looked at me, he had already understood everything.

"So, what have they proposed to you?" he said. "How do you know?" I replied.

"When you start doing something good, at first you make a lot of enemies who will try to stop you by discrediting you, then when they see that they can't stop you, some of them decide to be your ally. Since they can't beat you then it's better to have you as a friend, that's how you start getting constant job offers," he said.

"They made me a proposal that I can't refuse!" I replied.

"I understood it as soon as you entered this office looking into your eyes. Your eyes are too transparent, even when you try to be tough your eyes are too transparent. I know you're a good guy and you'll never be ruthless, you're a bit like me but remember that not everyone you will find will be like you and me. I know very well that your destiny is not to stay at this company all your life , but I would like you to stay here for a few more years. I'm not going to try to convince you by begging, you'll have to decide, before accepting my proposal. Think about it for another week. We'll meet again next Friday afternoon at 5:30, you'll have a week to think about it, I hope you will change your mind during this week"

I was a little confused because emotionally I wanted to stay and work with him maybe all my life, but I felt that if I accepted I would miss a train that maybe wouldn't come again.

I told Dr. Sbrenna that I was going to Milan to sign the contract one week later by inventing an excuse for family commitments. A week later I found myself face to face again with Alain in his office.

It would have been easy to walk into that boy's office little older than me but wise as an old man and tell him with a friendly tone"I have decided to stay!", but instead I said the most suffered "no" of my life. A few seconds of silence followed, I didn't have much else to add because the knot in my throat prevented me from talking. I wanted to tell him a lot of things, thank him for everything he had done for me, for turning me into a successful manager, a desperate guy who a few years earlier had shown up at his door just because he wanted to make some money to go and live abroad. He had somehow saved my life and I will be forever grateful for it. But who knows why, in certain circumstances you can't say everything you want.

He looked at me with a kind of smile and said, "I already knew your answer I just wanted to test you, if you really believe in what you do, don't get distracted by feelings, least of all at work. Keep feelings for private life, we may continue to talk as friends but if you decided to start a different career path, it's right for you to do so. It would not be fair if you stayed here just to please me. If you'd told me you'd stay and realized this isn't the right place for you anymore, I'd have to let you go. Then he turned to his white bookshelf, stared at some books, and then chose one. That book was

"The Zen and the Art of Motorcycle Maintenance," he opened it and wrote these sentences:

May the road come up.

May the wind always be behind you.

May the sun shine warm on your face.

The rain falls soft on your fields

and until we meet may God

hold you in the palm of His hand.

Many years have passed since that moment, but his charisma has not stopped accompanying me and every time I found myself in difficulty, one of my thoughts was "what would Alain have done if he had been in my place? And soon after I always found the right solution.

CHAPTER NINE

Life is made up of difficult choices,
many yeses and many nos
that determine what we will become.
Arturo Mazzeo

Milan is the most avant-garde and most international Italian city in Italy, where there is a constant air of modernity and innovation, a city that tries to keep up with the new world standards, a pity only that it is held back by Italy itself, because Italy is a country that has never been governed by people oriented to economic development; it is enough to look at the data and at the many young graduates and undergraduates that every year are forced to leave Italy, to look for a job based on meritocracy that can reward their real abilities.

All the new world innovations when they arrive in Italy pass first from Milan and then spread throughout the rest of Italy and often the new global trends especially in the field of fashion are created in Milan.

If a foreigner comes for the first time in Italy and only sees Milan he will have a completely different view of Italy from what is then the rest of the country. If Italy were all organized like Milan it would be a completely different country, a country at the forefront of

Europe and perhaps competitive on worldwide scale.

If you want to see the Italian style about fashion, just by walking the streets of Milan you immediately understand that you are in Italy, what you expect from Italy in terms of style you find it here, just look at the people on the street, and the shop windows and see the unmistakable Italian style, recognized all over the world. Those at the Munari Shoe factory had bet on me and I didn't want to disappoint their expectations.

I had set myself the goal of giving a more youthful imprint to their image, proposing to their designers alternative models for the foreign market that I had to manage. I wanted it to be understood in the market that something had changed in that company, and I wanted it to be understood that that change was due to my entry.

I started to travel a lot, the planes and hotels of the world had become my home, I often went to sleep tired in a city and then in the morning when I woke up I no longer remembered which city I was in. Business was going well and with the first earnings I bought the car that until then was only in my wildest dreams: a black Porsche 911 convertible with beige leather seats. But that hectic life was so different from the one I was doing before, and it hid a second face: loneliness. I'd stopped hanging out with old friends, and the new companies were just good for the time of a party.

Although during the week I was always surrounded by many people I met for work, deep down I felt lonely because none of them were particularly "warm". On the weekends, I would sometimes finish work and I wouldn't even go home. I stayed out in the cities posing as a tourist in places like Singapore, New York or Melbourne and I was almost always just wandering around or sometimes I would stay in the company of women I only met for sex because when I told them that I did not live in the city and that I would leave the next day to go home, every now and then they understood that with me they could only have a weekend adventure.

The people I met spoke only of business, about money, about cars, about boats, about women who meant nothing but sex to me, topics that only conveyed a great sense of emptiness to me.

After almost a year of that life, I felt in need of talking to someone who understood me and the only one who could do it was Alain. Alain who I hadn't spoken to for a long time because I had decided that I would only call him after I had something very important to show him, and I still did not feel ready.

When I went to London and New York, the people I'd meet every now and again would invite me to private parties that started late at night and ended at dawn. Parties where alcohol was used instead of water and cocaine particles were mixed with those of the little oxygen left in the room due to the smoke in the air. At the end of those parties it took me two days to recover completely and sometimes I would even arrive late to the Monday appointments.

When I was in Italy my new friends were the children of well-known Milanese industrialists who considered themselves rampant managers even if they stayed in the office only a few hours a day and the rest of the day they spent in the gym and in the tanning booths. When private parties were held in Milan, some entertainment and sports personalities were invited and some of the ones I met in person were very different from how they appeared on TV.

At one of those parties I met Emilia, a girl used to being courted by many men and for this reason she was one of those women interested in those who did not try it on with her, perhaps because you are more attracted by who you can't have.

When I first saw her, she didn't like me and I didn't talk to her much, maybe my disinterest drew her attention. One Friday night I was in Milan in the company of the usual group of friends including Emilia, at Club 61, a place that no longer exists, often mentioned in Vogue in those years. Carlo the director who knew us well wanted to impress Emilia and even if she understood it, he pretended not to understand. As usual, we had also been drinking too much that night, and Carlo also helped by offering us drinks to make sure that we would stay there longer. From time to time Carlo would approach our group to have a chat, even trying to be nice to Emilia. When most of us got up to go dancing and Emilia sat down, Carlo came up to her and after saying something in her ear he tried to kiss her but got a big refusal and a slap.

After receiving that slap in front of everyone Carlo called one of the bouncers telling him to take the girl out of the club because she was drunk. Having seen the scene from the dance floor, we immediately went to Emilia's rescue and left the club with her. Once outside we consoled her and told her it was best to go home, she agreed and approached my Porsche asking for a ride.

She lived in Brianza, in an area populated only by villas surrounded by immense gardens and trees as fences. At one point we got to a huge gate, she got out of the car and typed in a code, the gate opened and we continued along an unpaved road with huge trees either side, the house could not be seen immediately. We arrived in front of a huge old house that looked like a restored castle and she told me to park right outside the annex where she lived. It was a huge annex, consisting of five rooms with a lounge and a fireplace all finely furnished.

Since it was late night no one had noticed us, perhaps the servants who slept in somewhere in the huge house in front of me might have heard the roar of my Porsche and the dogs that could be heard barking from time to time in the distance. After complimenting her on the house and all that property I didn't expect to see, I asked her, "Sorry, who are your parents?"

"I thought you knew," he replied.

"No, actually, I was never informed," I replied.

"Maybe that's why you hadn't try to hit on me yet or you weren't one of those after me," she laughed.

-"Then who are your parents to have such a property? ... it's just curiosity ...", I asked her again.

" I don't care about my family right now, let's have some fun, tomorrow I'll tell you ok?" she said.

"Okay!" I replied, and we started kissing.

After about twenty minutes of making love in bed, she got up and headed to a piece of furniture, she took a box that looked like being full of make up, only that it was full of cocaine. She came back to bed holding the box and she said, "Have you ever licked a woman sprinkled with coke?", "No...!" I replied, and I accepted, not to disappoint her.

,A short time after starting this perverse game, I felt sick, my sight was clouded, the cold sweats started, I got nauseous and I was going to faint. As soon as I could I quickly rushed to the bathroom where I started vomiting. After I laid on the ground, I lost my senses for a few minutes, I wasn't sure how many. When I regained my senses I washed myself, drank water and when I got back to bed I found her on her knees on the floor snorting the cocaine left on the ground, I didn't know how long she had been doing it for and how much she had snorted.

Actually, at all the parties that had taken me abroad where they used coke I had accepted only twice and a very small amount, I smoked even more infrequently and few cigarettes because every time I would overdo it, then I felt sick, so I was not used to those substances. By then Emilia was out of her mind and you could see that she was not well at all, I was worried about her and I asked her to stop. "Look, that stuff doesn't do you any good!" I said.

She was lying on the ground and she had finished everything and was literally destroyed. I put her to bed, I stayed with her a little and brought her a glass of water. I didn't feel like I wanted to stay with her until the morning especially because she didn't understand anything anymore, I asked her if I could do anything and she just nodded no. I got dressed and even though she had fallen asleep I said goodbye to her and left.

The next day I woke up late and with a severe headache, I swore to myself that I didn't want to do things like that anymore because I wasn't happy with myself.

When I was out, I went to a bar and while drinking a cappuccino I picked up the newspaper and it was on the front page that I read, "Found dead suffocated by her own vomit, Cavendisci's daughter." Ettore Cavendisci at that time was one of the richest industrialists in Milan and Italy, his multinational business was present in various sectors from oil to real estate, and among other things he held fifty percent shares of the Munari Shoe factory.

Emilia was his daughter.

After reading that news, my blood froze and didn't know what to do, a thousand thoughts came to mind. I hadn't done anything wrong, I knew it, it wasn't my fault, but who knows what the investigators might have found or guessed since I was the last one to see her alive.

A few days later I was called in by the police for questioning, I told them the whole truth and despite everything, I was involved in a year-long trial in which it emerged that Emilia used drugs habitually and luckily they found out who was the person who sold it to her. Although I had nothing to do with that story and I was acquitted in full, my name was tarnished because I ended up in the papers among the suspects but unfortunately it didn't happen when I was acquitted fully. So, people only remember the first part of the news and that wasn't in my favor. Ettore Cavendisci, however, did not like the fact that he knew that his daughter was using drugs and even though I had no fault in that matter the management of the Shoemaker company no longer saw me in a good light. When I went to work, I understood that the atmosphere around me was no longer what it used to be and shortly afterwards they found an excuse to fire me. I was unemployed at the dawn of my thirty-two years, after three years spent around the world representing the Munari Shoe factory.

I found myself even more alone, without a job, without friends and at the mercy of a depressive breakdown. Even though I had achieved some important results up to that time, I felt like a failure, forgetting everything. I no longer believed in myself, I no longer felt up to it, I thought I wasn't worth enough, I didn't have confidence in the future anymore. At that moment what I wanted more than anything else was a shoulder to cry on, someone who could give me advice, who could make me believe in myself again. Having no one found, I found solace in music and motivational books, I was listening all day to music by Neil Young, James Taylor, Pink Floyd, The Beatles and reading Og Mandino's book "A Better Way to Live," I realized that the biggest mistake I haddone was that I spent time with that bad kind of people and I wasn't true to my values. I don't believe in "being tough", it's easy to be "tough" when things are going well and when you have nothing to lose, try to be "tough" when you suddenly lose everything. A man is defined also by his weaknesses.

Finding myself unemployed, the first thing I did was to sell my beloved Porsche but before saying goodbye, I told her inside me that we would meet again one day. The second thing I did was to study a plan to get me out of that situation. Unlike when I was twenty years old even though I had lost everything at that time I had a wealth of experience and knowledge that no one could take away from me and I had to utilize it. I had to focus on myself and do it quickly before the last of my financial resources I had accumulated dry up and I would end up finding myself at the mercy of nothingness and despair. At that moment I also felt abandoned by God, and the victim of a divine injustice, wondering why I had suffered the loss of all that I had built for myself, up until that time. I thought the price to pay was too high in comparison to the mistakes I had made.

But I soon realized that I had not been abandoned because in that apparent disaster there was another opportunity to give me another turn at life, thus following my destiny.

Sometimes to reach your true direction you have to go down some narrow and difficult roads, every change even those that seem like the end of everything are actually paving the way for a new opportunity that will take you in the right direction to which your life is destined to go.

CHAPTER TEN

There are no big prizes for small efforts.

(Arturo Mazzeo)

Sergio Collovani was a shy boy but full of ideas, I had him hired ine the marketing department of the Shoe factory Munari, when I was still one of the most important people in the company.

When he heard about my situation he phoned me, he was worried about me, telling me that the owner of Stanford Shoes in Macerata had disappeared leaving all the debts to his two daughters who didn't know whether to close the company outright or continue.

I had already heard that brand, it was a small artisanal shoe factory that produced well-made models but not up to date.

"James, this is the right opportunity for you to restart, I am convinced that with your ideas you could relaunch that shoe factory and make it great. Call him right away," Sergio told me.

I had nothing else to lose, so I listened to him, called and talked to one of the two daughters and set a date to meet me. I went to Macerata by train where the two Stanfoni sisters were waiting anxiously for me at the station. They saw in me as a lifeline for the fortunes of their company. It was a pleasant meeting, they had heard about me and had seen me at some trade show, so I didn't need a to bring along a CV or introduce myself.

The situation I saw was that of a small shoe factory, completely disorganized but still able to produce a very good product.

After the death of the owner, Mr Stanfoni, business had gotten worse as his daughters had no idea how to run a business, so things didn't look good for the future. As soon as I walked into the offices and into production, I immediately saw all the things that were wrong with it. It always takes someone who sees things from the outside, to understand your mistakes that you can't see.

It was a double-edged sword, you couldn't go wrong, or you would immediately bring the balance sheet in break even or shut down because the banks were no longer willing to extend their credit lines.

I recalled a phrase by Oscar Wilde: "A great artist doesn't see things as they really are otherwise he would stop being a great artist." In that condition, if I were able to take that company to the top I would have had a chance to relaunch myself and no one could say that it was thanks to an established company because Stanford Shoes at that time was nothing.

The two Stanfoni sisters told me at once that they couldn't pay me a big salary, it barely gave me a little more than what a clerk earned.

I accepted it. I found a furnished apartment paid for by them, I agreed on paid work trips and if I had reached the break even within a year I would have also received 5% of all the turnover I would have made from that figure onwards.

The two sisters accepted surprised by my enthusiasm and said, "James, we're going to trust you, if you can't make it in a year, we're going to close down and you're going to be without a job!"

I laughed and said, "I have nothing to lose, in the worst scenario I'll be looking for another job in a year's time!".

As soon as I took over the Stanford management team, I surrounded myself with four new young employees full of grit and enthusiasm, who above all had the ability to see things as they would become in the immediate future.

As big or small as companies are, they're a group of people working in synergy with machines, so you're always dealing with brains. People are always at the heart of everything, so in order for a company to be successful you must invest first and foremost in people. If an employee does not work with satisfaction it is at the expense of the quality of the product. A word of appreciation said at the right time, would make everyone part of the company's successes and everyone proud of the results.

I have often heard entrepreneurs say, "this employee knows how to do his job well, I'm lucky that he works for me but it's better that he doesn't know that otherwise he'd ask me for a salary increase".

It is wrong, however, to tell him would make him feel more gratified and make him work with greater motivation.

Dale Carnagie said that at the bottom, a pat on the butt is only a few centimeters away from a pat on the shoulder. I would add that this just makes the difference between a respected entrepreneur and a feared entrepreneur, the difference between the two is that the second will get from his employees only the bare necessities. The people who work for entrepreneurs who are only feared but not respected do so only for the lack of another job but if they receive another proposal, they will not think twice about changing jobs.

It is not true that no one is irreplaceable because each person is different from the other and everyone has something special and unique. When a company changes staff too often, it can discredit its image, it slows down the work, without also considering that for a period you must dedicate time training the newcomer.

Why are there companies selling more than others even offering the same product, price and service? Because it's the human factor that makes the difference. It's the reason why you choose to spend money willingly in certain stores while in others you no longer even enter. In some companies which lack of skilled people, especially dealing with the public, there are decreases in turnover.

So, do you realize how important people are in a company?

That's why some sellers or managers are so sought after and well-paid, because they have the ability to increase a company's turnover.

At Stanford, together with my team, I created a new collection that we launched with ads aimed at the new customers we wanted to target. I changed the position of the company in the market, I decided to sell to a young clientele, so I changed the product to please the type of customers I had decided to target, after which we started with specific advertisements with slogans that immediately gained attention.

At the end of the first year we reached break even, the result was achieved, we continued to grow and within three years Stanford acquired a new image in the market. It paid off its debts and became a nationally known brand with eye-catching collections that even the competition started copying and when someone copies you it means you're really succeeding. We were able to create models that stood out from the competition, the Stanford shoe was instantly recognizable and that's what I wanted.

I felt like I was just a step away from the clouds again, and at that moment I felt the need to call Alain to tell him everything that had happened to me in the last few years.

I phoned the Golden Shoes, she always answered, the secretary with a sensual voice but this time she knew who I was, and she was glad to hear my voice. When I asked her to pass me to Alain, she was astonished by me as if I had to have already known that he hadn't worked there for a year. He had moved to live in Brazil to start a new project that no one knew about. I asked her if she had his number or address so she could contact him, but no one else at Golden Shoes knew about it. At that moment all my enthusiasm ended, giving way to a feeling of sadness and melancholy. I don't know why but I felt abandoned, because even though I hadn't spoken to him for years, I knew he was there and that at any time I could call him or visit him but now knowing that I would never see him again made me feel deprived of my point of reference.

My greatest regret was that I could not see him again in order to share with him the fruit of his teachings. Since I had left the Golden Shoes, I had been successful, then I had fallen and once again I had risen to succeed and this, I owed to him, to what he had taught me.

I was convinced that it was not a coincidence to have known him and I remembered a phrase "If someone shows you the moon that is the one you have to look at and not the finger that points to it", paraphrasing that phrase, I would have liked to thank him for showing me the moon.

Two years later when I returned to my hometown, the city from which it had all started, I passed in front of Golden Shoes and was amazed that it had changed its name. I told myself to try to understand why and I learned that it had been purchased by a multinational company that was not interested in its brand but in its know-how. That multinational kept that plant open for another three years after the acquisition and then fired all the workers to move production abroad. From that moment it became a large abandoned factory, no one bought it, and the guys who enjoyed doing graffiti murals began to use the outer walls to have fun making their drawings. It was really sad for me, every time I returned to the city and pass in front of the Golden Shoes and see the conditions in which it was reduced to, a shoe factory that was once one of the most important artisanal shoe factories in Italy.

I looked at those old walls and remembered everything I had done there, I remembered the faces of the people who worked there, what happened every day inside, and then I thought if on the day I had made the decision to leave when it was still a glorious factory, I had instead decided to stay I would not have done everything I had done and I also would have suddenly found myself out of work as had happened to the other employees.

CHAPTER ELEVEN

Everyone dies, that's the thing
that everyone has in common
but not everyone really lives.

(Arturo Mazzeo)

Within five years, I'd been able to win it all back, maybe...

Success, money, a nice house, the Porsche model that I had had to sell years before and in the meantime during a trip to Canada, I met Dolores, the woman I married and who gave birth to my first two children Jasmeen and Terence.

All this well-being, however, soon made me dissatisfied.

A man dies when he has nothing left to desire: in fact, at that moment what I lacked was the desire to desire something.

When I used to dream of owning what I didn't have, I was trying to do it and this adrenaline gave me the cue and the energy to move forward.

At the time that I had achieved all my goals, I could no longer appreciate what was around me: I needed to experience new emotions again. Nothing surprised me anymore, everything seemed too obvious. At first, I didn't want to talk to anyone about it, I was afraid they wouldn't understand it, and I thought it was a momentary crisis. Behind the facade of a successful man, apparently satisfied, lurked an unhappy man looking for something to desire. It seems strange but I missed the problems to solve, I felt the need for the challenge with which I had always faced life. This restlessness again led me to get into trouble, to shake my life a bit I began to do random things: I drove recklessly and in addition to some minor accidents I was constantly fined... but it wasn't enough for me. I started making business decisions that my employees no longer understood... but it wasn't enough for me. I began to indulge in adventures in which I cheated on Dolores. I was putting my quiet life at risk; but deep down inside me it was what I wanted.

For years I had chased security and when I found it, I didn't like it anymore.

Continuing with this behavior I succeeded in my intent.

One night she was tired of seeing me depressed, she finally asked me what was the problem and then I decided to confess everything to her, I told her everything I was feeling inside and she understood that I had cheated on her. She decided to leave me and return to live in Canada, bringing with her little Jasmeen and Terence.

I couldn't blame her, and I didn't try to stop her.

The thing that hurt me the most was the detachment from my two children, as well as the tragedy of destroying a happy family.

Despite all the years that past, I learned how to build a friendship with Dolores and began to see my children often.

Jasmeen is the oldest of all my children, with her I have always had a telepathic relationship: she seems to be tuned to my mind, she always knows what I'm thinking and why I behave in a certain way, she is the only person in the world who really understands me. We found out just by being away: one day she phoned me from Toronto, it had been a week since I had heard from her, and as soon as I answered she asked me if the fever had passed. No one had told her that I had been suffering from a strong flu for five days.

Terence, on the other hand, has become my right-hand man, although in the past I have had a difficult relationship with him.

When he was a child, he saw me as something else, I was his hero, but growing up he began to see my weaknesses as a man and his myth collapsed. Over time I made him realize that no one is perfect, and he re-evaluated me as a man, becoming today my most valuable collaborator in the company.

The day I accompanied them to the airport as children when they left to live in Canada, I will never forget it because it was also the one that once again turned my life around.

It was raining so hard that the sky seemed to fall on me. When I saw them getting on that plane, my heart clenched and I knew I had got it all wrong, but it was too late. I wasn't proud of myself, to say that I felt like a bad man is not exact, maybe I was confused because I was sorry but I had not changed, I still felt within myself that desire to get back in the game.

That was one of the most decisive moments of change in my life, everything was finally becoming clear in my mind. The highway that was taking me home was straight, the windshield wipers set at top speed were not enough to clear the windshield from the rain falling from a sky that seemed angry with me. The wind blowing from every direction made my car unsafe and not stable, my car was about to stop, like others that had already pulled over on the side of the road. In that situation the only thing I could do was to be very careful and look forward, because if I got distracted, I would lose my concentration and risk drifting. If I had looked at the row of stationary cars along the hard shoulder of the carriageway, I would have put myself in real danger, a slight distraction would have ended my run against the side guard rail.

Maybe God at that moment had created that scenario to talk to me, he was showing me my life: he was giving me the answers I had asked for.

Everyone in life has a goal to achieve, when a man is born, he does not know what his destiny is, he must try to discover it by living day by day making his choices according to his actual abilities and aspirations. It's like being at a crossroads where there are so many streets without indications, only one of those can lead you home. If you choose to go the wrong way you will come to a place that, as beautiful as it may be, will not make you feel at home. You have to look inside yourself to discover your own aspirations, your own aptitudes and your limits. It is true that any route you choose to take will still get ot a destination, but if a person arrives in a place that does not belong to him, he will feel inadequate and dissatisfied.

We are free to walk and choose the path we want, the roads are all open, but if we choose to follow the one that does not lead us to our goal, we will never feel satisfied.

So, here's how to figure out if you're fulfilling your destiny or if you're going down the right or wrong path, you already know, just listen to yourself and how you feel inside.

Each path is different because each man's abilities are different, so everyone in life occupies a different place and a different role.

As I was driving on that tormented road, God was showing me other cars who had to stop because they could no longer continue, it was making me realize that if I didn't concentrate I could end up doing the same, even if my objective was to return home. Even if everyone has a goal to reach it is not obvious that you will get there, depends on how motivated you are to get there. You have to earn your own destiny.

I had to continue on my way regardless of what was going on around me, regardless of the choices that others had made.

Everyone has their own story it is wrong to compare yourself with others. In those car drivers stopped at the side of the road, for example, I saw those old friends of mine who discouraged me every time I stated I wanted to do something important in life.

They wanted me to believe that they gave me useful advice for my own good, they actually gave me certain suggestions because they didn't want to see me doing something better than them.

That night I slept soundly because I had finally realized that my life was not meant to be spent as a flat line, always doing the same things. I felt like I had to get back in the game and the only way to do that was to get by on my own, create my own company and risk everything I had again.

CHAPTER TWELVE

*We become
what we think.*

With the money I had set aside and the liquidation I received leaving Stanford; I was able save enough capital to open my own company. I came up with a name: West and Belt, which means nothing, but I liked how it sounded, and this became my brand with which I would express all my creativity.

At that moment I was leaving a certain job for an uncertain one, but I thought "after all what is really certain if not death?".

I have always thought that there is no such thing as real safety. Safety can be achieved relying only in one's own abilities, only this can be the base to build one's own future. Work will come knocking the door on its own, if you know how to do something well. That was the moment when I really felt like I had nobody to fall back to, alone against everyone, and I was risking everything I had firsthand.

The adrenaline of the old days came back and I finally began to desire something, this was my real gasoline, the desire to get something through my new company. Every now and then I would think of a phrase I had read in a book: if a man does not have the courage to risk everything for his own ideas either he is not a great man or they are not great ideas"."

I had clear ideas about the type of product I would create and propose in the market, and what kind of positioning I wanted to achieve, this was the most important thing, more than the capital I had available. If you have a large capital but you don't have a clear idea of the positioning you want to achieve, you will end up losing all the money by doing the wrong marketing and you may even go bankrupt. The first thing you need to start a business is to have a clear idea about the positioning that you want to achieve, thinking of the potential customers in the market, after clarifying this aspect then you will know what kind of product to create, with what features and price.

I also knew that I had to start with baby steps, my philosophy was: to start small thinking big. What could help me grow, who were the kind of collaborators I would surround myself with and the quality of my product. In one of the books I had read it was written just this: "the other person is the source of our satisfaction. Those who seek admiration, respect or love, can only obtain them from a relationship with others, things and objects cannot give anything that lasts. Only people can offer what we want, so it is important to understand them and to do so you need to strive to understand yourself." I chose five young people with a basic level of experience and those made my first staff team. We were all in agreement on the kind of work to be done and soon our first collection was born. After many years of market experience it was normal that I already knew many customers who immediately trusted me as soon as they knew that I had created my own brand, so I did not have much trouble fitting into a market saturated with offers.

In conjunction with my launch on the market, a disparaging and defamatory campaign against me and my new company had also begun, started by some of my old competitors who feared that I would take away a slice of their turnover. But I had taken it into account and my answer was the same as always: silence. It was the right answer in fact and in the long run those who plotted against me put themselves in a bad light on their own.

For the production of my models I only chose top-notch material, although I knew that this would affect the final price of my shoes, but the positioning I had chosen for my company was a medium-high level clientele. The only way I could fight against the big market giants was to make shoes that were taken care of in the smallest detail that they couldn't do. My shoes really made a difference, nobody else was using the leather I chose, they were shoes that could last fifty years, and the real shoe enthusiasts understood it immediately. I invented models like I had done before; with the companies I had worked, aiming for a specific style. My models had a very specific identity, they did not resemble those of the competition, I wanted that in time someone would try to imitate me and I would not have to imitate someone, I bet on this philosophy and I was rewarded.

"West and Belt" gained prestige earlier than I thought and a fair share of the Italian market in my customer portfolio.

The real turning point, was three years later in Paris when at a fashion show, where I was present as a simple spectator to try to understand the new trends, I met Helly. She had just finished shooting her first film in the French capital, she had been cast because still being an unknown actress she was cheaper, but she was able to play whatever role was proposed to her. It was a blast, we had unforgettable days, we both knew that everyone had a different life ahead of us. Upon her return to the United States, I made her forty pairs of shoes as a gift, the entire summer-winter collection of the "West and Belt". Her reaction was immediate, she immediately phoned me to thank me, swearing that sooner or later she would find a special way to reciprocate, but I had done it in a selfless way.

Two years later, during the Academy Award, a television program that interviewed all the actors present at the awards ceremony gave a long interview to the Oscar-nominated actress for Best Female Lead. Responding to a question about style, she stated that Italian style was her favorite and in particular, she loved Italian shoes and that her favorites were those of the brand she was wearing that day. The camera repeatedly panned down to her shoes and showed off the gold WB initials engraved sideways on her black velvet stilettos. They were among the most expensive and sophisticated models in my collection. That night, she was awarded the Academy Award for Best Actress in a Leading Role: Helly Strendall.

It was the most profitable free advertising in history, at least as far as I'm concerned. From that moment on, in every photo shoot, Helly wore "West and Belt" and American buyers started sending me orders. In a short time I was overwhelmed with orders, turnover increased by 120% and I had to increase production, work round the clock, hire new staff and form new collaborations with subcontractors, because after the American market followed orders from the European, Asian and Russian markets. "West and Belt" became a status symbol of luxury, and to maintain this status among the other things I did, I increased the prices of each shoe even more, also because we were full of orders and we weren't caught up in the urge to sell.

When I realized that the "West and Belt" were present in the best luxury boutiques around the world, including Harrods and

Selfridges in London, I knew I had made it.

In the following years I opened new boutiques in the main streets of Milan, Rome, Paris, London, Lugano, New York, Zurich, Los Angeles, Miami, Moscow, Shanghai, Hong Kong, Tokyo, Sydney, Madrid and Denver. I found new designers among the most talented in the industry who I paid more than my competitors paid, not to give them the idea of switching to the competition.

Helly became my official spokesmodel for three years, after her followed the best models of haute couture who felt flattered by the proposal to represent the "West and Belt".

After eight years of growth my company had reached a turnover that if one day someone had told me I would have thought it was a joke, and I never in my life imagined that I could achieve an economic well-being that I enjoyed. At that moment I decided not to expand further but to dedicate myself more to the philosophy of quality: to improve the quality of my shoes and at the same time the lives of my employees. I wanted all my staff to receive a higher salary than, to make them feel a part of the company, in this way they would work with greater responsibility and care for the product and this would be beneficial for my production.

I didn't want "West and Belt" to become a mass product, it had to stand out from all my competitors and produce something not accessible to everyone. There is nothing wrong with this, in any market there are products accessible to all and products accessible only to a segment of customers. There are those who aim for a mass clientele producing a price oriented product, made with less valuable materials and those who instead choose to make a very well-groomed product, with very valuable materials, marketable at a high price and therefore accessible only at a "high end" market share.

Instead of paying a higher than normal salary to my employees, I could have hired new staff but paid everyone the basic salary, but if I did, I would not have achieved the result I had set myself.

I have always stated that man must strive to improve his quality of life: having succeeded for mine, I felt compelled to do something for others. A person content with his salary would come to work with more dedication and would consequently put more care into the production of my expensive shoes. Those who bought my shoes had to know that that quality product was produced by people who care about quality and who were paid well. If, on the other hand, my customers had seen that my shoes were produced in a factory located in a country where salaries are very low, they would have felt ripped off after paying four times more than those of the competition.

What could many employees have brought to my company instead, simply being treated as numbers? No one forced me to do what I did because law provide a set salary for all kinds of jobs, but by sticking to those laws, I wouldn't get the same results.

This philosophy proved me right, in fact I soon noticed that the factory was always kept in order, if I asked someone to do something beyond what they were required to do, they did it happily without feeling exploited, also when walking in any of the offices or departments there was a feeling of serenity. The quality of my products could also benefit: fewer and fewer imperfect pieces were sold as second-choice items.

At the age of forty-seven I met Sharon, but for fear of making the same mistakes of the past I did not have the courage to marry her. It was proposed to me to buy an estate in France, near Cannes, when I saw it, I fell in love with it right away. It had been a while that I had been thinking of moving and that I thought I needed a change of scenery, to live outside the place where I worked. I was lucky enough to be able to follow my business even from afar, without the obligation to go into the office every day.

So, I settled down with Sharon at Villa Chambrì, where within four years Penelope and my fourth son Richard were born.

Penelope has always been the most rebellious of all my children, she never wanted to listen to any of my advice. She has always criticized my lifestyle: she wished she had had another kind of father, one of those always present, work and family. I have not yet been able to create a friendly relationship with her, despite numerous attempts, on the other hand I have always left her to be free to make her own choices.

Richard, on the other hand, is an artist, plays piano and guitar, composes songs and expresses himself with other art forms such as painting. Like all artists, he lives in a world of his own, sometimes he goes quiet for days not because he's angry with someone but because if he thinks of something new and doesn't want interference.

In front of Villa Chambrì, attached to the estate there was an old disused annexe, full of junk belonging to the old owner.

The day I decided to clean it, I had initially delegated that task to my gardener, but since the plane I was supposed to take that morning had been cancelled I gave Jordan the gardener a day off and I decided to do it myself.

There was old furniture, ruined curtains, broken plates, rusty cutlery, gardener's boots, torn clothes, time-faded photographs, a boat engine, branded cards, dusty books.

The only thing that had been preserved in a decent way was a large painting, a portrait.

I cleaned it well, curious to see the face of the person who probably must have been the old owner of the villa. He was a man in his forties, with a distinct air about him, slightly grizzled black hair, a hint of a smile and a bewitching look. He was portrayed half-bust, posing in his office, wearing a blue jacket, white shirt and red tie. Behind him there was a huge antique bookcase full of books and the family crest, a red lily similar to the one Alain had tattooed on his right wrist.

In his gaze and in his face, I immediately recognized something familiar: he could look like a relative of mine even though I had never seen that man before. Shocked by what I had just seen, I went to call Sharon who when she saw the portrait asked me if it was a joke. I had to get to the bottom of it and I started doing some research that led me to meet the last retired butler of that noble family who told me everything.

It was a noble house fell in disgrace due to the penultimate of his descendants who had never wanted to modernize the family farm and then by the son of the latter who loved gambling. The last of the descendants, when he was thirty years old, decided that he was going to start working, he invested the money left in the jewelry trade. He knew how to do business but had the vice of gambling and despite being married and having a five-year-old son, he still loved to frequent the nightclubs of the French Riviera and neighboring Italy. It was in Italy that he met an American girl who had won a scholarship to study directing with the famous director Federico Arganti. It was the first time Eduard had lost his mind to a woman. The wife immediately filed for divorce when she learned from a private investigator, she had hired to stalk her husband, that the American girl was expecting a child.

Before leaving, his wife demanded a large amount of money and in return would leave custody of her son to her husband. Eduard was very attached to his son and in order to keep him with him he decided to sell the villa to his wife, who a few months later sold to a wealthy Arab for a considerable sum and moved to Lyon. Eduard, on the other hand, no longer had ties to France and having lost everything, he moved with his young son and the American girl to Imperia with the intention of creating a new family.

After the birth of her new son, however, she only had a few more months to live with her new family before Nancy's illness took her life. The girl's name was Nancy Jaspersen and gave the child the name James in honor of her favorite actor: James Dean. Upon her death the child was placed in an institution and was soon adopted by a couple who could not have children. Eduard knew nothing about his son, but he remained alone with his first son Alain, with whom he tried to continue living, devoting himself entirely to the jewelry trade.

The work can have the same function as a bottle of spirit to make you forget. Eduard was not a good father, he had great remorse for what he had done and tried to lift himself up with work, which is why he neglected Alain who was raised by a housekeeper and when he was old enough to leave he did not hesitate to do so.

They were both too proud to apologize, so in their lives they continued to see each other infrequently. Eduard Feret died at the age of fifty-seven of cirrhosis, alone in his small house in La Spezia where he had moved the last years of his life.

The police found him, alerted by the neighbors, suspicious of his television that had been on continuously for five days and the strange smell coming from his house.

So that's how my real biological father died.

CHAPTER THIRTEEN

*The rewards in life are
at the end of each journey,
not at the beginning,
and we cannot know
how many steps are
needed to reach the goal.*

(Arturo Mazzeo)

If on the day I discovered my father's portrait I had taken the plane I had booked, I probably wouldn't have come to find out anything. Isn't that weird? Maybe not all of them are coincidences, maybe we are part of a plan that must inevitably come out at the right time. Everything in its time, you just have to wait for the time to be ripe for everything. If I had taken the plane that day, the gardener would have cleaned up, thrown everything in the trash, without dwelling too much on who might be the face of that portrait.

Instead that didn't happen, my flight was canceled, and I came up with the idea of replacing Jordan in the cleaning of the outbuilding.

If I see it from a spiritual point of view, I believe that my father had done everything to make me meet Alain who taught me many secrets in order to succeed in work and then that I could buy that villa, his old house; then he created the conditions so that I could clean up that annex, so that I could find out the whole truth. Maybe he wanted to apologize to me... he had succeeded.

There comes a time in life when what we dream becomes what we do, life is made of cycles, ups and downs, once a cycle ends immediately follows another.

The cycle I never wished I had to live was the end of my relationship with Sharon. Damn the party where she met the man who took her away from me.

It was a very difficult time because this time I didn't let it end, I thought we were going to be together forever. I was fine with her and I never thought that this feeling after eleven years of living together could change.

I spent a long time wondering where I went wrong, then I realized that blaming myself was no use. I thought I knew her.

But how can we think that we know a person well if we don't know ourselves well either?

Before leaving, seeing me downcast and far from the strong man I used to be, she said to me, "But James, weren't you the one who said you didn't believe in eternal love?"

She told me this because I once told her that I did not believe in eternal love, I had defined it as a feeling of complicity through which one can spend your whole life next to a person.

It is sad that after the first period of falling in love that feeling of infatuation so strong that you do not get sleep, eat and be yourself, slowly fades until it stabilizes in a beautiful feeling with which two people between ups and downs continue to be together.

In my previous relationships I had always done everything I could, as long as that initial phase of infatuation lasted as long as it possibly could because I never enjoyed the second phase.

I often wondered if it is right for a couple to continue to be together if love has turned into affection or friendship.

In such a situation it can happen that every now and then one of the two falls in love with another person and lives that love clandestinely, for fear of hurting the partner, for not having the courage to interrupt the marriage or just in the pursuit of the thrill of the forbidden fruit.

I have never liked to see a couple who are together just because "they are together", many couples after years continue to be together for many reasons: for fear of loneliness, not to be alone, for fear of not being able to find another partner, for fear of hurting the other by leaving them, for children, or for the public image. But I think the only reason to continue to be together is only if at least one flame of love has remained and if you still feel happiness looking into your partner's eyes.

It is difficult to determine after so many years whether that feeling is still love or has turned into something else, often you prefer to continue to be together so as not to create a new problem trying to understand what you really feel.

Sharon took her suitcases and sent them to Verona, to her new partner's house, the next day she picked up a car but at that moment I wasn't at home, I had decided not to see her again. I felt hurt, overtaken and defeated by another man and that hit me. I was suffering from the idea that at that moment she could be happy with another man instead of me, while I still didn't have anyone who could really replace her in my heart. I consoled myself with the women who were there at the time, better to say that they served to give me only a little pleasure, it was like smoking a cigarette or drinking a glass of Japanese whiskey. But that wasn't what I was really looking for, but you can't replace a love overnight.

When you are rich and known if you remain single it is not difficult to find women to keep you company, but at that time I wanted to be a perfect stranger to find a woman who would appreciate me only for what I am, without thinking about the advantages that she could have by being with me.

That research lasted two years before I understood that I would only find what I was looking for if I stopped searching for it because if you approach a woman with the air of those who are desperately looking for someone, you can only find three types: a woman in the same condition, and then she will not worry too much about understanding how you truly are, because she just needs to have someone next to her; an opportunist who will try to figure out if being with you will be like winning the lottery; one interested in an adventure but only for one night.

I didn't want any of the three.

CHAPTER FOURTEEN

Norman Vincent Peale once said
he only found people without trouble
when he visited a cemetery.

I've always thought that life is a matter of viewpoints.

I admire some people; they value others who they think are a step above them and so on; you could continue indefinitely.

It's a chain that will never end because there will always be someone above you, it all depends on the perspective you are looking at it from. Today I feel like I live in a fairy tale: I have realized much more than I imagined and I am living inside a dream: what I thought was impossible when I was still caddy, is now reality and this is enough to believe that things happen if we make them happen. If we believe in it, we are well on our way: our willpower and tenacity will attract other aids, visible or invisible.

The first step is to remove that wall of mediocrity from our minds that others have built or rather those who do not have the courage to dare.

The biggest problem facing society is not fighting delinquency or drugs, but the concept of mediocrity that has spread, feeling mediocre, creates enormous damage to society every day.

Thieves steal because they don't feel capable to achieve what they want with their skills; rapists rape because they do not feel able to conquer a woman and the only way they have is to take one by force; drug addicts become that way because they do not feel up to the task of dealing with life's problems.

Those who feel mediocre and have stopped facing the first obstacles now live a life that they did not want, that does not belong to them; they took the wrong path that did not lead them to their goal.

Mediocrity creates masses of people who unite to feel stronger that together make a damage that individually they would not have made. Beware, therefore, of those who have failed to fulfill their dreams, those who tell you phrases like: "In life only the recommendations matter", "don't dream too much", or "only a few succeed" by implying that you will not be among those few. These are some of the phrases that would make you feel mediocre, spoken by those who feel so. Remember that it is not a disgrace to have tried and failed, it is a disgrace to have given up in the first place.

Many people think that only those who have reached the highest level, should continually update themselves, but this is not the case. Everyone should be updated: both those who work as a freelancer and those who work as an employee, because being up to date also means knowing how to hold a conversation about modernity. How many people talk just because they got their ideas from someone else? They are people without ideas, who do not study, don't update themselves and end up being a harm for society. People as such tend to believe to the first revolutionary phony leader who will never be able to deliver what promised, and just get the power from ignorant people who don't update themselves. Think about the damage an unprepared leader could do? He will end up being in the control room, taking decisions that will influence millions of people and that could collapse a country. All this can happen just because of ignorance, due to people who don't fact check what they hear. It may sound farfetched, but believe me it can happen.

One of the habits I have never lost is to meet personally the young people who work for me.

When I ask if they are happy with the work, I often hear this reply: "Yes, but if I could have a promotion, I would be better!". Then I answer by asking them what they are doing in order to get the role they would like. Most of the guys tell me that they are not doing anything to improve their position, they wait for the right opportunity but in the meantime, time passes, and the opportunities are slow to arrive.

As a qualified person I do not simply mean an educated person but someone who has the ability to put their skills into practice, giving a new and original imprint.

We must aim to become an irreplaceable person, that is, to know how to do something like no other can do; this applies to both the worker and the great manager. To achieve this, the keyword is: "training."

The saddest thing is not knowing what to do to create the opportunities of life. If you are not lucky enough to find a good teacher you have to educate yourself, slowly climbing your way up, also working for free at the beginning, just to "steal" the secrets of anyone who is more experienced.

You should not immediately expect to earn lots of money as a professional. It's just a matter of time, everything happens at the right time. The formula is: "learn, apply, demonstrate and then ask", at that point and only then you demand.

CHAPTER FIFTEEN

Whoever has received, must give.
Nothing really belongs to us.
Everything was given to us
momentarily on loan.

(Arturo Mazzeo)

I was sitting all alone on a rock in Porto Venere on a September morning looking at the sea and the endless line of the horizon when these words came to mind: "Whoever has received must give, nothing belongs to us, everything was given to us momentarily on loan", I felt in debt to life. I felt that I still lacked something to accomplish in life.

I had managed to become a good salesman first, then a good executive, eventually becoming a successful entrepreneur. What was I still missing? What I had was a gift to share and pass on: the only way to do this was to teach young people how to realize their dreams. I gathered some good managers and professors around me and "The Dream Shop" was born, my training school.

I wanted to unite professors and managers because in my opinion, certain notions if explained only by those who have spent their lives teaching, are not as convincing as those explained by those who apply them every day in the practice of their work.

A lot of unemployment is due to the fact that young people today are no longer willing to work in the so-called "humble" roles because anyway when they get home they always find a hot meal.

Another reason is that there is little by way of specialization; I am not referring to the master's degree of the University but to the ability to actually do a job.

An unemployed man who was hired by a company in most cases would not be able to actually do the job immediately. For this reason, very often when an employer needs qualified staff, in order not to take risks, it seeks them within other companies: this means that looking for work without being able to prove that you will bring a plus to the company will certainly be an even more difficult task.

Always put yourself in the shoes of those who have to pay your wages, since

it is always difficult to choose; we will focus on who will prove to be up to a specific role. Contrary to what you might think, it will certainly not be by saying "I'm ready to do anything as long as you hire me" that you will be able to convince of your validity. It is certainly better to say that you specialize in a specific job, this is the most convincing way to make it clear that you are not an all-rounder but a specialist. Better to know how to do only one thing well than doing many but badly.

Once, in order to work you were ready to emigrate to other parts of Italy or to distant lands, just read the story of America or Canada, it was made by emigrants. Today, very often in Italy, there is no protests about the lack of a jobs because there are many offers for manual labor that are not taken in consideration. Very often they protest to demand a job close to home, well paid, which does not take all day and if possible, one in which you do not work weekends. The unemployed protesters also complain about social inequality, wealth which they believe is not shared equally without bearing in mind that life itself is about meritocracy. Apart from those rare few who inherit a fortune or win the lottery, whoever can buy luxurious things that others can't get, succeed because they have been able to create the conditions to get them, so they deserve it. You don't earn as much based on the number of hours a day you work otherwise a line worker or a clerk of a cleaning company that works so many hours would be rich, but based on the wealth you can create. A manager earns a higher than average salary because he makes money and improves the company he works for and by expanding, they can create new jobs, so they also help to create wealth. A sportsman earns a lot because he has visibility, because when he plays, they entertain millions of people watching him live and from home, and that makes money move. No private company would give large sums of money to someone without having a bigger return.

When a company decides to pay a person well, they have decided to make an investment in order to earn more and does not consider it an expense. So, if you want the same salary as a successful man, don't be an all rounder, be a specialist, and try to do what he has done to get there. Prove that you deserve the salary you have asked for, showing that through you the company will earn more, otherwise you will have to settle for a basic salary or little more. Always try to stand out from the crowd, with training. Only if you are more well-trained than others can you succeed, the world is for those who believe.

It's easy to protest when things go wrong, to feel like victims, but this is the wrong way to deal with things, focus instead on possible solutions and you will see that you will be able to move things in your favor. The first step is, stop feeling like a victim!

Being driven not by the greed but by the passion, I decided to fund my training school "The dream shop" entirely. My purpose was only to help those who were really zeroes, those who wanted to start doing something good with their life but did not know the right strategy, who were really determined to trace his or her own path. I entrusted the management of the West and Belt to my son Terence and devoted myself for a time to my new enterprise.

The press did a report on me, defined that choice as a business strategy to make them talk about me and in favor of the West and Belt, they didn't immediately understand the true meaning of the initiative.

I am convinced that if I had retired to play golf around the world, I would have had more admiration and benevolence.

I didn't want my training school to be mistaken for a master's course for managers, I just wanted to take care of ordinary people, training all those kids who were facing the working life for the first time and didn't know how to achieve their dreams.

I found their names in all those job advertisements and had them contacted through my secretaries, once I had made the initiative aware, I invited them to participate in my course for free. I did not promise them a job or recommendations, but by putting into practice what they had learned they had to find their own way and little by little to be able to climb the top of the success they had set themselves. They didn't have to get rich because success is not judged by money but by achieving their dreams and it's not always about money. My course was based on the philosophy of how to discover their potential and exploit it. I've always thought that if you want to help someone you really don't have to feed them because soon after they'll be hungry again but teach them to earn food like and they'll be able to feed themselves their whole lives.

At that time, I started dating Denise, a thirty-one-year-old girl who managed to amaze me with her simplicity. She was not immediately accepted by my children, almost aged the same as her, but after getting to know her they had to think again.

It is precisely in the mature age that I have been able to give myself completely to a woman.

From my twenties to my fifties I focused on professional affirmation and in trying to understand myself, after that age it is as if I had returned as a child, I found myself more generous with my attention and more attentive to appreciate even the small things in life.

Since I've been with Denise, I have rediscovered the desire to do sports, I'm careful with what I eat, I have more free time, plus those who know me well say that lately I have a more youthful appearance.

At the age of fifty-nine, I felt very satisfied with both my private and professional life, so it was natural for me to leave more and more space to my collaborators, often retiring to enjoy the silence of a small castle, bought in the hills of green Umbria. I have always been fascinated by the mysterious legends that revolve around castles. One day wandering like an aimless tourist through the Umbrian countryside, I discovered a lovely castle very well preserved but turned entirely into a hotel restaurant. Fortunately, its owners were tired of being hoteliers and when one evening at dinner almost as a joke I asked them how much they wanted to sell it for, I agreed on the price, and the castle became mine. First, I closed the restaurant and the hotel, bringing the castle back to a simple dwelling. The castle of San Petronio is truly an enchanted place, it seems that time has stopped on those hills. Standing still for hours reading and admiring the landscape was a cure for the soul. At times like that, it seems impossible to me to think that one day I will no longer be a part of this world.

I don't think life ends with the death of the body; it would have been senseless to live. I have seen to many evidences that made me think that one day I will continue to exist under another form, the more I grow old and the more I go on, the more I feel part of someone's project.

I think ghosts exist because they didn't want to go and leaving enchanting places like St. Petronio Castle for good. The peace and quiet of this place, however, have not erased that desire that I rooted inside to travel and to feel like a citizen of the world. I dreamed of a place where I could take refuge to spend the last years of a past life without feeling the need for a permanent home. However, I had not remembered the words of Alain, that one day he told me that in my life, I wasn't meant to retire.

In fact, after almost a year spent at the castle in the company of Denise, one day I felt the need to get back on the line. It seemed like my New York business office couldn't make without me, and I couldn't live without it.

Staying at the castle made me mature, the idea of writing this confession book, perhaps to apologize to my children who did not see me when they needed it most. Reading this book, I hope they understand who I really am and why they saw me so little. I spent years all around the world doing business deals, trying to become who I am now without realizing that I was losing the most important things in life: myself, my affections and my years.

I have known heaven and hell, I have done things that I am proud of and others of which I am ashamed, but each was the reason that made me what I became. I spent years thinking that it was only right to do things that did not change over time but everything is born in a way and then transformed, every moment of the present is worth living it right away, without waiting or thinking that the right one will be tomorrow.

I have never hidden a wrinkle because it is the evidence that I have lived my years fully, it is right to live every age with its transformations and accept everything it gives us, beautiful things and bad things because one thing generates another. Whatever happens is the result of a previous action, so everything is a consequence of what we've done before.

I've always been sad for some young people who think, "I don't have to do this otherwise when I'm old I might regret it", as I think, those who think like this don't need to get old, because mentally they already are.

I have spent years without knowing that basically, you live even just to see a sunrise or a sunset, it is wrong to identify life only with work, there are days when the right thing to do is to rest, even reflect and meditate means to live.

Knowing that I still have so much to learn gives me new drive, this makes me feel alive.

Many older people of a certain age think that this is now all they could do, or they have done it all, and having no more stimuli after a few years, they get sick and die. They self create their disease because our minds can also decide our health, it is our minds that also command our immune systems, in fact when we are stressed we are more prone to illnesses because our immune defenses are low, or when we are afraid our belly hurts.

Every religion teaches what is permissible to do and what is a sin. if we instead evaluate what surrounds us with a parameter of judgment different from what they inculcated us as children, we will discover new truths. It should only be our conscience that decides what is really right or wrong to do for each of us and choose the right religion for us or to decide not to follow any of them. However, it is difficult to make this choice because we are not really free to judge since society imposes its rules and parameters on us and not everyone has the courage to break away from the rules of society. In order to be able to judge freely, our consciousness should first cleanse from all that it had absorbed since our birth and create new parameters of judgment based on what each individual truly feels inside.

I couldn't create a traditional family, maybe that wasn't the reason I was born for, or it could have been my failure.

Now I wonder if it was life that gave me a lot or if I deserved everything I had, but you can also think that life was so benevolent with me because I won its esteem. To live convinced that we have an answer to everything means to have walls in our heads, our brains are not designed to be able to understand everything.

Writing is not like talking, you have more time to reflect, to think, to correct, I used this medium to grasp the meaning of what I have done. With this summary of my life I tried to leave a part of me, I do not want that my passage on this planet, to be like a footprint in the sand waiting only for the wave that will erase it forever.

CHAPTER SIXTEEN

*The opportunities are often so small
that our eyesight cannot distinguish them
and yet they are often the seed of great feats.*

I found this book in my father's desk drawer, although it was a very intimate confession as you could read, I felt it was right to publish it, since one of his philosophies of life was to try to leave a mark.

Now I'm going to tell you how things went from the moment my father finished writing the story of his life, so you'll understand why from this moment on the writer is his daughter Jasmeen Jaspersen.

It was a beautiful Sunday morning and we were in Monaco, James was sitting on the dock in front of his boat, named after Venus the Goddess of Love, looking at the horizon with his gaze completely lost in the void.

There was a bright, warm spring sun, a light sea breeze had just arrived, stroking her face, causing her short-grizzled hair to move.

A stereo somewhere near was playing Elvis Presley's song "He'll Have to Go," James loved that song like the whole Elvis record and got excited.

Suddenly he changed his expression, he seemed to be troubled as though he had learnt some bad news, but he wanted to hide it. It was his birthday; he was sixty-seven years old and maybe that made him feel old... I wonder. I had a strange feeling, but I was afraid to admit it.

All four of his children had come there to celebrate his birthday, all together. Something we had not done in a long time.

James had been waiting for that moment for so long that and he cared so much that he had arranged everything meticulously according to his style, leaving nothing to chance. We had lunch at the restaurant below the Hotel La Nuit Rouge, both of which he owned: a seafood menu, paired with a slightly sparkling white wine that for ten years has been produced in Provence on the Jaspersen farm estate.

At the end of the meal, my brothers and I insisted that we go to the private family suite of the Hotel, where James lived when he was in Monte Carlo, to give him his gift. As soon as we all entered together, I placed my hands on the bandage covering his eyes, and a few seconds later removing them from his face, James found himself in front of a red package that hurried to open. He was a man you couldn't give him anything to that he didn't already have, the only gifts that could excite him were the symbolic ones that could only be made by those who really knew him.

The package contained a white uniform, original of the U.S. Navy we knew the special relationship that tied it to the sea, and this moved him.

With his eyes shining with emotion, he immediately wore that white uniform that was well in tune with the soft tan of his face. "This is the most beautiful gift I've ever received! Not only because this uniform is beautiful, but because a gift like this could only be given to me by those who know me deeply, so it has double value. These are the things that make me feel truly just a step away from the clouds!" he said, and he hugged us in one embrace. Four faces so similar to his were cuddling him, who had a nose like his, who had the eyes like him, who had his same expression, but looking at us all together, you could tell that the four of us were siblings.

After the thanks and the beautiful words, he proposed we all go for a walk on the beach. As we were coming out, he stopped me by the arm and said softly to one ear, "You understand that I feel like something is wrong today, right?"

"Yes Dad, I don't know what this strange sense of sadness is, and that makes me even more afraid," I replied.

"You know, Jasmeen, I have always been sorry and at the same time pleased that you had this sort of telepathy with me. You have always felt what I felt, that's why you were closer to me than anyone else," he told me. "I know Dad, I understand the reasons for your choices, I really knew how you felt at every moment of your life and I know how you feel now. You should just be happy, you're fine, you're fit, it's a beautiful day, it's your birthday, all your kids are here to celebrate you, and yet there's this sense of sadness. At this point I'm afraid something might happen to you but know I won't allow it!" I said.

'Don't worry, it's just a bit of passing sadness, nothing's going to happen, Jasmeen. You know everything has two meanings: the most obvious is the one that we can understand right away, the second is too big and perhaps even the most important but to understand it takes time".

We went to the beach where we walked and played around on

the sand like children, he was not behaving like our father but as one of us. Time had flown by and it was seven o'clock in the evening before anyone had even realized it, James looking at his watch and knowing that Denise would arrive at nine o'clock that same evening at Cannes airport, told us to get ready to pick her up at the airport.

Ten minutes later we were all ready to get into two different cars, but James changed his mind telling us that he would go to Cannes by sea aboard his boat and from there he would take a taxi to the airport.

"But dad, what's the point of doing this now? Come with us..." we all told him, but when he had an idea in his head it was hard to make him change his mind.

"I want to put on the uniform you gave me and go aboard my boat, so if there's anyone who wants to come with me, they are invited to board!" he said.

"But dad, you're going to take a lot longer, come in the car with us," we kept telling him.

"No way, just take me to the marina, you'll see me set sail, you'll wait 20 minutes and pick me up at the port of Cannes so I'll avoid calling a taxi to go to the airport," he said.

We knew that it would be pointless to keep trying to convince him, so we escorted him to the marina where we helped him board his boat Venus. He wore the white uniform, took off his shoes and put on a pair of boat shoes. He hugged us all as if he were about to go on a long journey, then he told us to strike a pose and we took a group photo with the car.

By now the sun was beginning to set and we were starting to see a bank of gray clouds coming, bringing a downpour maybe, so we said for the last time, "Dad it is going to rain, are you still convinced? What's the point?" He hurried to turn on the engine and unhook the knot that kept the boat docked at the quay.

After unhooking the boat and leaving the harbor he hoisted the sails and turned off the engine, accompanied by the rustle of the wind that pushed his boat, he watched the coast become smaller and smaller, as we also saw him become smaller and smaller and I at that moment began to cry. Terence, Penelope, Richard and I began to drive towards Cannes divided into two different cars, suddenly we heard a loud roar burst into the sky, very strong lightning, which foreshadowed the rain. The wind started to blow much stronger, it was a very strange and sudden atmospheric phenomenon. The few boats at sea began to return to port as fast as they could, but James by now had gone too far out, he continued to head towards Cannes in the waves that began to get higher and more impetuous. James had launched another of his challenges, this time to the sea forgetting the first rule that a sailor must never forget: never challenge the sea because it will always win!

We stopped and got out of our respective cars and looked towards the horizon and cried "Daddy, Dad" while knowing he wouldn't listen to us, this time from a distance.

Our screams were lost in the wind and they received no response from that stubborn warrior who alone was challenging an army of waves. We rushed to call for help but the coastguard could not get out immediately due to the sea conditions, so they sent a helicopter to his rescue, but it had become dark.

Hours and hours of endless searching in the dark on that rainy night, flying over the sky and fighting against a kind of hurricane that did not seem to stop or at least decrease.

They continued the search until dawn before surrendering, neither James nor his boat was found.

The next day the weather had returned to normal and the search continued, the seabed was also searched with special small submarines in the hope of discovering something, or at least finding out where the boat had sunk and being able to recover the body, but again no trace was found.

This time, the valiant warrior James Jaspersen lost his last battle, this time giving the enemy the most precious thing he had: his life. Two months after the incident, we the children were summoned to New York, where lawyer McDester opened and read the will he had received in custody a year earlier.

It's been five years since Venus led her commander to the clouds.

Testament

If Lawyer McDester is reading this letter now, it means I'm no longer with you. It would be better to say that I'm no longer there physically because even if you can't see me right now, I'm there next to you. First of all I want you to know that I have had a beautiful life and I have very few regrets, I hope that what I have been able to build from nothing is not lost and serves as an inspiration to those who at this moment feel alone and lost, without a penny but would like to succeed in achieving their dreams. Money is not the fundamental thing to begin with, the most important thing is the right ideas, for this reason disclose my history and my teachings, in the hope that they will be able to help someone.

Hi Jasmeen! I know that right now you feel close to me, and you are crying! Please wipe away those tears!

That direct thread that unites us hasn't broken yet, and it's never going to break even though you can't see me.

Hello Terence! I'm sorry I didn't tell you many times, even though I tried to prove it to you with the assignments I gave you. Often a good word can be better than a gift, so right now I tell you that you are very good. When you still need me, call for my help and you will get it.

Hello Penelope! I hope you've forgiven me for not being the

father you wanted. Know that I've always loved you the way you are even when you were away from me. Keep doing the kind of life you want, I'm proud of you. I want you to be happy doing what makes you happy whatever it is.

Hi Richard! Thank you for the times you named me in your songs! Keep it up, creativity is a beautiful gift, music will reward you and it will never make you feel alone. If you listen to your heart, we will write your next song together.

Whatever you want to do in life, do it now; tomorrow is not tangible, tomorrow does not exist, tonight you could die, anything is possible, the only sure thing you have is the present. Tomorrow, if it exists, is a consequence of the present, what you will have tomorrow you owe to the present.

I have never been afraid of death itself as an event, I have always feared disappearing before I have accomplished my mission and have left a trace of my existence.

I was afraid not to realize something that could give me a legacy, now I am quiet because my legacy is you together with the things that I have created and that will continue to exist even without me.

The goal that has always given me the drive has always been this, and when I reached the awareness that I had achieved, I felt a step away from the clouds.

Now that I have arrived in the clouds I feel neither hot nor cold, I am neither hungry nor thirsty, I feel no fatigue, I am no longer afraid of anything, there is no day and night and not even the sense of time.

Everything is becoming clear before my eyes, a clarity that cannot be explained to those who are not here.

You have wept for me only because you do not know the here you feel free and light, suspended in the clouds.

At first, I could not believe it, I never imagined that it would be so easy and painless, now there is nothing on earth that I would change for this.

You are still here but remember that every time you open your eyes you have another opportunity to learn something new to put to good use, this is everyone's job, it would be a crime not to do so.

Every day can be unforgettable, make sure that it is, live every day as if it were the last.

Never think: "I'm going to have fun tomorrow," "I'm going to do it tomorrow," do what you can do tomorrow.

Don't even think: "I will be happy only if...", you must be happy regardless of any event; try to be happy even when everything seems lost, even if I know very well that on certain days it can be very difficult or seems impossible.

Make no comparison between the days: each one could be the last, so live every day of your life with this awareness.

Do something every day that will make the day worthwhile, and before you close your eyes, always ask yourself, "What have I learned again today?"

Imagine this: what would you do if they told you that were going to die at midnight today?

Surely after the first moment of panic, once you became aware you would try to do what you have not yet done in your life, and at the end of the day you would be amazed to see how many things you have managed to do, and you will think that if you had behaved like this every day, you could have achieved much more in your life. Make the most of your abilities and enjoy the things I left you because you were luckier than others in this life.

Now you must grant my last wish.

Donate sixty per cent of the money to the "No Man's Child's House", it is a charity institution that takes care of all orphaned children, it is the Institute where my adoptive parents found me.

The remaining forty percent will divide it into four equal parts, the Cannes villa, the Hotel, the restaurant, the castle of San Petronio and the other possessions will be of common use.

Surely considering the inheritance taxes, property maintenance and investments that will be needed to continue to run the "West and Belt" profitably, your share will not be enough to be able to live off, doing nothing with your lives, and that's not what I want for your own good. Did you think I'd let you live on an inheritance? If I had done so I would not have loved you, because I would have taken the meaning out of your life.

You will be forced to make small sacrifices that are certainly not comparable to those that a miner has to make every day.

You will learn that you will need to exploit your cunning and intelligence, setting yourself goals.

It does not matter what you are today but the goal towards which you are moving, is what one of my masters said, it is better to have little but gained with your own forces than getting much has a gift.

What satisfaction would there be in being gifted a fortune?

When life will weigh on your shoulders and you feel too weak to carry the weight, breathe a sigh of relief by thinking that at the end of the day this is just a moment, a drop in the sea of eternity.

I will be close to you even from up here, even if you cannot see me, I will be with you at any moment, I will never abandon you.

You can feel my presence among the books I read, peeking through my notes, listening to my favorite songs, driving my car, spraying my favorite perfume in the air, playing the strings of my guitar, entering my office, sitting in my armchair or just wearing one of my sweaters.

I will be with you as often as you think of me, every time you dream of me and when you enter an empty and silent room you will feel the inexplicable feeling of not being alone.

I will be with you and you will find out when you understand that it is not for a series of coincidences or by sheer luck that certain situations will solve for the best. I will be there, I will always be there and as long as you look inside yourselves you will find me there, alive, caged in your heart. Nobody really leaves.

Your father.

James Jaspersen

Printed in Great Britain
by Amazon

41686626R00078